FOUR SEASONS OF MEMORIES

Precious Gems

By Olga Garcia

This book is dedicated to

My family

Thank you for your support

In FOUR SEASONS OF MEMORIES Seasons' End a story seems to have ended. Sometimes love doesn't end, with a story. Does a love story continue with Guy and Darla? Meanwhile there's no turning back, Art has published, Precious Gems. Mr. Scavo has drifted into sail, while leaving Guy to work alone with investments. Won't be any easier to own. The grown-ups have made up their own world, but their children refuse to go unnoticed. Is it, they play fair? All seems as if Mona has been left single. Will she find love again? Characters we know play in Precious Gems, new ones play in as FOUR SEASONS OF MEMORIES becomes, Precious Gems.

FOUR SEASONS OF MEMORIES

Precious Gems

FOUR SEASONS OF MEMORIES

Precious Gems

"Guy, I don't always understand what you do, why?" Art was in his office.

"You've found out, Darla and I have been seeing each other. Is that it?" Guy walked to a friend from his desk.

"I, uhm, have since remarried my, wife Carol." Art said.

"A marriage that should have never ended." Guy said. "Glad you understand that."

"About you, and?" Art asked.

"Hm?" Guy looked at him without answer. "Art, being the best friends we are, I'm sure you don't need me tell you, who that is I'm talking about. Friends, like Oso and Guy, Uzma and Art."

"Congratulations, Guy. You've gotten that one signature, owning it all." Art said. "Sea Lance, who's the owner is, questioned now."

"Always knew you a friend I could trust." Guy smiled. "Your boat will have priority, with me?"

"Thanks. I'll make sure, I follow every rule." Art walked out the office. "Greg, not the best friend, to anyone?" Art walked in Greg's office.

"Art." Greg was front of Carol in his office.

"Art, just walked in Greg's office to say, hello." Carol turned to look at her husband.

"I went to congratulate the boss Guy. Owner of all this, and well more." Art said. "Forgive us, Greg?"

"Your wife, both in love." Greg understood.

"Carol, you know how this ends?" Art said.

"Art?" Carol asked.

"With you and I, together?" Art said.

"Afraid, Carol, doesn't follow but your work." Greg said.

"Ah?" Art said. "You've not published it, into your work?"

"It's probably every word comes out your mouth, Art, have owned it." Greg smiled. "It's not that easy to be copycat."

"Haha." They laughed.

"Say, hello to whoever it is you're dating now, Greg?" Art walked out his office with his wife.

"I, uhm, will soon as I find her?" Greg alone in his office walked to his desk.

Art and Guy are at Sherese and Corbin's home often...

"Grown-ups think, it's their world." Sage and Guy are invites.

"Sage, will you forget about it?" Guy was done tying his shoes. "We have our own world."

"If you say that, I believe you." Sage kissed him. "So, someday we'll visit them? Like my parents?"

"Let's go." Guy smiled in a hallway.

"Let's go." Sage in a hallway closed a room.

"Where are you going?" Art is also at Sherese's home.

A home has a kitchen behind staircase to each side a dining room. Right side one for an everyday meal, and another for special occasions...

"You guys are going somewhere? Sherese is done with the kitchen, asked for breakfast?" Corbin walked in a living space to the left of a home.

"My parents miss us." Sage apologized at the door. Middle of a home.

"Where are you going?" Sherese walked out to the door front center of a home.

"Can't go anywhere, without explaining to family." Sage smiled at her husband.

"On your way out." Guy arrived at his parent's home.

"Dad." Guy son walked out the door.

"Guy, have a good day." Sage walked to their car.

"Same." Guy walked in the house.

"Where's Magda?" Sherese asked at the door.

"Guy, I keep sending your boys home?" Corbin said at the door.

"Oh, no. You keep on inviting us to live here." Art smiled also at the door.

"Sherese, breakfast." Corbin walked to the dining room right in the home.

"What I'm here for. Magda, would have breakfast with friends." Guy said.

"Magda, is more of a friend, than she is, a wife?" Sherese sat at her place at the table.

"Hm? Who, isn't?" Guy asked.

"I hate to say it, Guy?" Sherese said. "Sometimes," She put her hand over her napkin on the table. "I believe, I've made a mistake. Then, I tell myself, that's impossible, God never does?"

"Haha." They all laughed.

"But, might have Darla, been the girl for you? You know, without all that..." Sherese looked at Art who was at the table and Blair who'd just walked in the dining room.

"Good morning." Blair sat at the table. "Did, I interrupt something?"

"Grandma Sherese was just apologizing to dad, about Darla. Wasn't the best mother-in-law." Art said.

"Sometimes the wrong parent, is the real one." Blair smiled at Guy and looked down at her plate.

"Ah?" Everyone looked at her.

"I suppose, I've been wrong, before?" Corbin ate. *"Must be, I'm not god?"*

"Haha." They all laughed.

"Thank you, Blair. I really should call you about it?" Guy said.

"We all like the simple truth, papa." Blair smiled.

Hours later. Guy's boat...

"Can't believe, one moment we're at my parents, another we're on ocean." Sage smiled on a boat.

"We've had family vacation. We deserve own couple time." Guy smiled. *"Want our love to survive, all that isn't."*

"Guy, because of you, I believe in love." Sage smiled at an open bar outside the boat. *"Don't let me find out, you ever cheated on me?"*

"What, if I did?" Guy asked.

"Guy?" Sage laughed.

"Haha." Guy and Sage laughed.

"But that, break?" Guy said.

"Just know, I never cheated on you." Sage asked. "My heart always got back to you, soon something brought me back to, memories of us."

"Hm?" Guy smiled. "Why I love, my girl. You'd never look at my best friend."

"For that fact, your brother." Sage did say.

"Sage, you know nothing happened between, Nina and I. Will you forget it?" Guy asked. "What happened between you and me, meant so much more. This love we share, we've learned together?"

"Find out what love is. A couple sharing everything like two best friends, like lovers. We'd love each other the same, if we had lived some simple love?" Sage asked.

"Love, never a simple thing with a girl, like you, Sage." Guy kissed her.

Darla and Randy, are they having problems? In Randy's office...

"It's back to work, at my office." Darla said.

"Why do you continue to work. I'd think you'd be on your own with that writing by now, Darla?" Randy asked.

"Randy, don't just write for Four Seasons of Memories, I do lots other things. Like boss?" Darla reminded.

"Knowing you close to, your ex-husband, makes me a bit nervous?" Randy said.

"My ex-husband. But, Randy is my husband." Darla said.

"I understand that. It's not that I don't trust you, it's Guy I don't trust?" Randy said.

"Randy, we've been together enough years. You know, I'd never even dare think of cheating on your love for me?" Darla said.

"Hm?" Randy in his office thought.

"Randy?" Darla asked.

"Yes?" Randy asked.

"Appeared to me, as if your mind wasn't here?" Darla said. "You know, feels like that lots of the time? I talk to you, and you don't answer, to a question, comment I've made. You're not thinking about another girl, are you?"

"Hm?" Randy was in thought.

"Randy, will you please answer me?" Darla asked.

"I was, uhm, thinking about work." Randy walked to his desk. "You're right, we should get back to work?" He gestured to his desk.

"Right." Darla said. "You won't kiss me before I get back to my office?"

"I'm sorry." Randy walked around his desk.

"Randy?" Giana walked in his office.

"It'll have to be at another time." Darla walked out the office.

"What's wrong?" Giana asked Randy. "She's not found us out?"

"Giana, I'm sorry about dinner last night." Randy apologized.

"So, you had dinner with Darla. Understandable, she's your wife. We've only, just kissed a memory?" Giana said.

"Hm?" Randy looked at her.

Mona and Art remember moments from a past...

"So, Guy walked in my hotel room that day." Mona said. "Told me, he couldn't forget, how you and Darla were together. She cheated on his love. And I told him, while you're thinking about, Darla, I'm thinking about our past. Wondering if, it's possible, someday it will be pasted back together. He said, I'm not Desmon, I know what I want. Only, who I want seems to escape me? I asked, and that who you want, is Darla?"

"You should have walked out your own room, at Blue Bay, by then. But, you stayed?" Art said. "What did he answer?"

"He didn't." Mona said. "Haha. But I found out?"

"What, Mona?" Art asked. "Only dare to ask, because the past I know between you and he, know it love?"

"Art, I can't talk to you about this anymore. Haha. Hate to break your heart, with my truth?" Mona said.

"What you found out you could paste another moment, creating uninterrupted love?" Art was front of her as if confronting her.

"Yes?" Mona tried to laugh. "Was gone the next day. Darla was back in his life. Everyone heard about meetings, he'd begun presenting again. No matter what he said, was about he and Darla. When I called you, and you'd begun working for me."

"You're right, Mona, maybe it's true, we'll no longer be friends." Art said. "Honest hurts?"

"Does it, Art?" Mona asked him. *"Sherese, once asked."*

"Hate to ask?" Art asked.

"Carol, is your wife. You might want to remember that. She might get the wrong idea, when we talk. Hate for her to think, I give a ring, no importance?"

"Why a divorce." Art said. *"You know, people might end up killing each other off?"*

"Ha?" Mona laughed. *"That humor of yours?"*

"Haha." They laughed.

"Mona, I know you love Guy. Someday, you two will be alone, somewhere. I can't be there for you, all the time. So, when you're alone there with Guy, anywhere, some Island Cruise? Out on ocean, all to yourselves, will you remember, me? Will you see tears I've cried, because of this impossible love? Why isn't it just as fair? It's impossible love, for you two, now? You two deserve it, to find out just how much impossible love hurts?"

"Art, you're laughing about it, now?" Mona said.

"I am, but not about you and him, staying away from each other. You gotta care for another human being. Magda?" Art said. *"Cause someone's tears?"*

"Much as, anyone cares for my own?" Mona asked.

"Ha, bigger than that, friend?" Art asked.

"Someone's gotta cry someday." Mona said. *"That won't be you, will it?"* She walked to her desk chair.

"Cause, you've cried?" Art walked to her desk. *"Mona, someday you'll understand, it'll be your chance at love. Will be, who you love, and, uhm, uninterrupted."*

"Will it, Art?" Mona asked. "Because someday, instead of praying we'd end up married, I prayed I took care of business, before we married? To this day, I think, must have been the wrong prayer. Maybe we could have taken care of, it all. Love and Business?"

"It's too soon to talk, woman." Art smiled. "Heartbroken."

"Haha." They laughed.

"I'll let you know, if I've found love. You know, Greg was nothing more than a mistake." Mona regretted. "Wasted time. Desmon who I've loved more than anyone, he was my husband. Also a mistake. I'd hate to believe in love. Another mistake in, my life?"

"Then you got a date; but a date gone wrong?" Art smiled.

"I recognize those words." Mona smiled. "Haha?"

"Wolf." Art didn't smile.

"Mona, you'll tell me about Dragon someday?" Dario had walked in the office.

"Ah?" Mona and Art turned to look at him.

"There's nothing to talk about, Dario. Dragon and I had met. Before you walked in my office with him. We were, uhm, old friends?" Mona said.

"Yeah, way I hear conversations here and there. No one dare talk to me about it. I've just walked in on one, again. Dragon's intention with you, was never a friendly one. Nor, sequester for the money?" Dario said.

"No, it was all but a romance novel, Darius." Art said.

"You know, my criminal name." Dario smiled at Art.

"But, are you one?" Art asked.

"Your word against mine, Art." Dario whispered.

"Still, Darius, it is," Art walked three steps from Dario. "your word, against mine."

"Let's just hope this isn't sword against sword?" Mona said. "Haha. You'll end up finding out." She closed a folder. "Life, in prison."

"Hm." Dario smiled. "Am I a tell?"

"You know, someday I turned in a folder, as I do when my investigation is done." Mona said at her desk. "Sumae, walked in that office. And, asked, 'You've just paged that folder, I'm sure. You got it yesterday?' I told her, Sumae, I did just page it. As soon as I saw it involved a grown man, and a child, I dare close the folder the moment I read the child had said, yes. Sumae asked, 'Why? You'd think that is reason for investigation.' I answered, Sumae, sometimes courts waste their time. Children someday become grown-ups. They're no fool again, to be told, who they are. I'd read enough." Mona said. "But you're are both grown-ups. Know exactly what you're getting yourself into, should."

"One of us, does." Art insisted about innocence. "Mona, you're both not in against me?"

"Haha." They all laughed.

"One knows exactly who the world would believe." Mona stood at her desk.

"Ah?" Dario and Art looked at each other in trouble.

"Hm." Mona was an abiding citizen.

"Enough with the playing. One doesn't feel the same, once the cards have been turned." Dario laughed.

"Dario, life isn't a story. You may, make it up?" Mona did scold. "A liar, has allowed to walk this world without finding out, there is such thing, as—"

"Fact." Art said.

"There you go." Mona said. "We've been told, by our very parents."

"Ha?" Dario looked at them. "You don't all believe, I'm in this with, Wolf?"

"No one has said anything, about wolf." Mona said.

"No, one has, but I'm sure this all has to do with it?" Dario said. "Art, what do you know?"

"Nothing." Art said. "Rumors, probably as much as you?"

"Hm?" Dario looked at Mona. "Mona, sometimes in life, isn't you want to tell on people. You, must. How else could one help you?"

"Darius, finding out you're more than tell?" Somra walked in the office. "Sounds like, this is more than a tell to you?"

"Sometimes feels, like story, doesn't do enough?" Dario sighed. "Art?"

"Feeling the pressure, already." Art said.

"Guys?" Mona looked at them. "I've forgotten the whole situation with Wolf, think you all should too?"

"And, when you think someone else, could be going through the same thing, Mona, is story enough told?" Dario was front of her. "Wouldn't you rather think, your tell has a heroic reason?"

"Hm?" Mona looked at them. "Thanks, guys. Think I do enough around Detective's P I, still feels like I will never repay all you've done for me?"

"Mona, its lunch time. Guys, do forgive me?" Somra asked.

"Thank you, Somra." Mona walked out the office with Somra.

"Art?" Dario looked at him. "Art, more than a friend in Mona's life. You know, you may help her, with this? Around the office, one might make a mistake. Wolf couldn't have possibly made a mistake? No, his intention was to get attention. Might, Dragon forget sometimes attention, is attached to, prison? When one needs, a friend."

"Dario, I'm Mona's friend. I must respect her decision for quiet, what she really wants. Maybe, this thing you have with Dragon, is, uhm, just, personal? He's done something to you?" Art asked.

"I don't want it to become personal, someday, Art? I might not have family, I do have friends?" Dario said. "Personal matters, I can handle myself. Others, I'd need some help? Art, Mona is all she is to you, don't forget she is my boss. I changed my life around, long time ago. Had no idea, it'd become responsibility? Turn, crime in?" He faced away from Art still in Mona's office. "You know, I've betrayed crime life?"

"What one, must do." Art looked at Dario. "You've seen Mona. This isn't easy for her to talk about. She's decided for Somra."

"Somra is a friend, that understands her. Is his job, save her when she needs saving. Sometimes, to have saving, you must walk through fire?" Dario said. "What a courtroom feels like, for a criminal. Can't imagine a—"

"Victim." Art said.

At a restaurant at Blue Bay Hotel…

"Somra, thank you, I'll be fine." Mona sat at a table in the restaurant.

"Mona, I missed you on my ship." Lance sat at her table.

"Thank you, Lance. I've become a case to my friends. You know, I never wanted that. It's the reason why I've come on vacation to your boat. I like being seen as who I am. And, you know all that I've been through?" Mona smiled.

"What is it, with your friends?" Lance asked.

"They'd like me turn Wolf in, with all his crime." Mona said. "They think, Wolf is danger, not only to me?"

"Do you?" Lance asked.

"Can't be so heartless, if you've not done it before?" Mona said.

"Ah?" Lance looked at Mona. "It's all up to you, Mona. Then again, maybe he's been turned in with crime, with other victims? I've seen how this affects you, would like to avoid it all?"

"Thank you, Lance, you seem to be the only one that sees my soul, once you've looked in my eyes." Mona said. *"You know, feel like there's no one in this world that could not only love me, but understand me, like you?"*

"Desmon." Lance reminded.

"No, one." Mona held his hand. *"Desmon, dare deny anything's happened. Can't say, he didn't believe enough to pay ransom."*

"But, I?" Lance said.

"Yeah, well there was still pay for that tell?" Mona smiled. *"Think, story is enough sometimes?"*

"Why?" Lance asked.

"A victim, tires of fighting, Lance. May a victim, be tired enough to be forgiven to stop fighting at some point? Story, does remind, what victim, means. When, all out there inside that cabin, feels like a world, you only, once knew."

"Mona?" Lance held her hand. *"There is no one stealing you away, but I?"*

"I'll have vacation again, someday." Mona said. *"Haha. You won't get rid of me, soon enough."*

"Haha." They laughed.

"Slow, I might be, you never did give up on me." Lance said.

"Haha. You left me no choice." Mona laughed.

"She's allowed Lance, friendship?" Art walked in the restaurant with Dario.

"Maybe, hurts lots less. You know, the love of your life?" Dario dare say.

"Dario, I have a wife?" Dario said.

"Well, some of us, dare have two." Dario found a table and sat down. "Maybe, we allow Mona forget the whole thing. Her psychologist has showed up?"

"Haha." They laughed.

"What is it, he cures, heartache?" Art didn't smile.

"But, Art? Married man?" Dario reminded.

"Haha?" They laughed.

"Looks like you have all your friends, here." Lance smiled.

"Oh, those friends, just want the story." Mona said.

"And, you're a writer." Lance smiled. "I've read your work. It's, uhm, good."

"Thanks." Mona said. "It's not told enough, with restriction."

"Haha." They laughed.

"Dario was nice enough to allow those talks, over the phone." Lance said.

"Lance, let's erase that from our lives?" Mona asked. "I believe, we'd been interrupted?"

"Haha." They laughed.

"Lance, still cheating on me with, Mona?" Vienna sat at the table. "Wolve, is he in enough trouble, already? With the wife?"

"Ah?" Mona and Lance looked at each other.

"Sometimes, we mustn't forget the past. Remember it; Avoids it happen, again?" Vienna said.

"Sometimes, takes jail. Then they have understood." Lance said.

"Why do they let them out anyway? You'd think they'd lock them up. Haha. Throw away the key." Mona said.

"It's not kill, we talk about." Vienna said.

"Victim, would question that. Am grateful, I'm alive." Mona smiled.

"Mona, wouldn't like to be viewed as a, case." Lance smiled at his wife.

"Mona, sometimes victims feel the need to do something about it. There's no shame in that." Vienna said. "Sometimes only victim can understand, victim. You know, Wolf can talk lots, only when front of victim, might just quiet?"

"We have programs for that, Vienna." Lance smiled.

"You might like to be called, one?" Vienna drank coffee.

"Ah?" Mona and Lance looked at each other.

"I'm sorry, am I playing the wife, right now?" Vienna asked.

"Haha." They laughed.

"I know, me and Lance play around too much at the office, like we weren't working." Vienna said.

"Believe it, that we call it, work." Lance said.

"Haha?" They laughed.

"Difference, is love." Vienna held her husband's hand.

Back at Mona's office. A window is straight from an entrance door. Left in the office is Mona's desk. Mona and Art talk center in an office...

"I tried to allow you see, I was in a same restaurant." Art said. "But what I'm most hurt about is, Lance, has what an exclusive, of what happened to you? Cause, that can't be friendship, he's come looking for?"

"You're wrong about Lance, Art." Mona said. "Our friendship might extend to... Lance and I were friends. Our friendship was interrupted, he must find out why. He made his own investigation, on what happened to me. I was taken to a faraway cabin. I kissed a cop, when he came looking for me. Cop instead of handcuffing me, taking me in, he kissed me back. Dragon came to the door looking for me with the other guns, and took us both in."

"What?" Art asked.

"Yes, Art, wasn't the first time, Wolf had taken me away." Mona said. "Next time with Dragon's warning of, I better not intend to tell again... Another cop came looking for me, us. I dare kiss him too. This cop, put me in handcuffs took me in. Wouldn't hear a word I said. At the station, they finally believed me, why I had kissed a second cop?"

"Kissed, him? Them? What for?" Art with hands on his waist front of her asked.

"I don't know, Art. Haha. He was cute?" Mona said. "So, he would cry out to all his friends, cops. Handcuff me, take me away? They all came looking for the cop that was sequestered just the same. The cop, for evidence left his gun, had now joined

the gang, before catching himself dead... He'd left his gun under the bed, had been my room. Everyone knew he was alive and with them. As I had told them."

"So, then what happened?" Art asked.

"They've escaped all this time." Mona said. "First time, didn't do anything to Dragon. Keeps changing his name, friends."

"But that cop?" Art asked.

"That, cop, has become one of them wolves." Mona was sure. "Believe me, I was insulted, he didn't holla about that kiss?"

"Mona, you're a beautiful woman." Art accused. "You'd get away with anything?" He questioned her.

"Now, Art, you'd accuse me, the same, if I'd done anything to survive?" Mona cried.

"Mona, we get alone badly like this?" Art apologized.

"Now why weren't you that cop coming after me? Haha. Least, I gotten to kiss a cute one?" Mona laughed.

"I would have turned you in, just the same, cutie" Art said.

"You aren't kidding, either." Mona said.

"Haha." They laughed.

"Mona?" Lance walked in the office. "I came here to see how you are, but you're obviously, fine?"

"Haha?" Mona and Art turned to look at Lance.

"Mona, would you like me to leave you alone to your office?" Art looked to a computer.

"I was hoping my men and I would come together against crime?" Mona smiled front of them. "Darla's."

"Why Randy?" They asked Mona.

"Think this has become more than my own problem?" Mona questioned.

"Why Randy, he's no cop?" Lance said.

"You do know everyone." Art said. "Could be a detective?"

"So, it's everyone's problem." Mona said.

"Has become." Lance said. "That's just not good for Wolf."

"Mona, I know you're going through lots… Friends, need to get back to an office?" Art questioned looking at Lance.

"Art, we should be here for Mona?" Lance said. "Let's not make this about us?"

"I'm a married man, Lance. I'm sorry, you pretend I'm just a complete stranger on your boat, thought it'd be the same, around here?" Art asked.

"I'm sorry?" Lance apologized. "Mona, what would you like us to do?" Lance asked.

"It's what Sumae asks me all the time. I dare ask, 'I thought you were boss?'" Mona laughed. "Know guys, I turn in rape cases all the time. But, when it comes to what happened to me, I can't even spell the word? Think it's time we came after, these wolves."

"Mona, been?" Art asked.

"Guys, hope you are." Mona asked.

"I'm hoping the cop is playing them, right to jail." Lance said.

"I doubt that, cop was having too much fun, to call himself innocent." Mona said. "He enjoyed, sending me right back to my room, after each meal."

"That's what a criminal does, is what he must portray?" Art said.

"You really believe that?" Mona asked. "I'd like to have faith, in someone? I mean, I did, trust a cop, while I was there. Never did they catch us, not fighting about something? Like, 'Why would you kiss me!' and 'Why would you not handcuff me, take me away!' And, 'Well it worked, didn't it? I got myself in trouble?'" She explained.

Miles away...

"Back at the office." Jimmy said. "Your story did save us. Mona in question about that story."

"Yeah, some undercover you had to put yourself through. Only so they'd investigate, what else would we say? Yeah, you were sequestered. All part of the game, you'd play along, you knew nothing, Mona said nothing?" Wolf said.

"Yeah?" Jimmy was in thought. Was he still undercover?

"Nathaniel, cried wolf, like a good cop does. But, Jimmy, did he? Time Mona kissed you, Jimmy. Nice try for her if she cried innocent about me in that room." Wolf laughed.

"What, about?" Jimmy asked.

"You were in that room, enough time talking to her, not to tell you same story. She told all my guys. Rape." Wolf said.

"Oh, come on, maybe it was part of her plan. She was brought in. We knew we were caught then." Jimmy laughed. "We had to run out that cabin, hide. Now, you can't go sequestering girls, making them your girl, Wolf."

"It was love, cop. Only happened with Mona." Wolf said.

"Just be careful, with Italiano. Been after him for a while to know he's no real cop." Jimmy said.

"What are you talking about?" Wolf asked.

"When he makes a kill, never turns it in. Think that's suspicious enough. Even when right, he'd be in trouble in the courts. That evidence. Why he doesn't bother with it. If you ask me, he's got that drug purchase all wrong too. Bringing it someday, to sale? Keeping profits?" Jimmy said.

"You've been working yourself too hard. Haha. Suspecting your own people." Wolf said.

"I've warned you." Jimmy said. "So, I had to work myself into crime to get away from you. Wolf and your gang. But, Italiano, think he's just bad. Kind doesn't take any."

"Italiano." Wolf said. "Think he could be boss over me."

"Isn't?" Jimmy wasn't sure.

"Just worried, I've fallen in love again." Wolf looked at a girl they'd sequestered.

"If she's not intact, they'll not pay us, what we've asked for." Jimmy reminded Wolf.

"Think that will be, worth it." Wolf said.

"Wolf!" Jimmy pushed him.

"Ooh, are you still playing your cop roll? You forget, the moment I asked you quiet about being in that room alone with Mona, you did." Wolf said.

"Wolf, Cobra, no matter what you name yourself, when the come after you, you won't need no name." Jimmy said.

"I'd like to entertain with you. But I got to see that girl. Before they take her away." Wolf walked away.

"That wolf is gonna get us in trouble?" Jimmy pointed at him.

"Hm?" Everyone shrugged.

"What's going on?" Italiano walked to them.

"Nothing." One of the guys assured.

"Keep a close one, on Wolf." Jimmy said. "We want a full amount, we all need to get paid?"

"Hm?" Italiano worried looked to the room where the sequestered girl was.

In the room...

"What do you want?" Gene got up from the floor.

"Just want to talk to you." Wolf got close to her.

"I have nothing to talk to you, about. If it's not that you'll let me free?" Gene cried.

"Ah, why would you want to be let free, instead of joining us?" Wolf asked. "We could—"

"Wolf?" Italiano walked in the room.

"Italiano, how many times must I tell you, to knock?" Wolf asked.

"Wolf, you have to know, someday, you have a new boss? Stay away from the girl? She's getting us that money? All that money." Italiano was front of Wolf.

"Step back?" Wolf said. "I know what I'm doing. Don't need someone breathing down my neck?"

"We had a cabin, you made us run from it?" Italiano said. "I can't keep on allowing you another home, and another?"

"I can get them myself?" Wolf said.

"You can rule your gang yourself too. Cops will sure come looking for you. Cause, I'm not in?" Italiano said.

"How can they be sure, you're not really in?" Wolf asked.

"Cause, I'm not." Italiano reminded. "You, remember that, you know they come asking about me?"

"Hm?" Wolf didn't answer.

Italiano is in his office...

"One tries to do as one must." Italiano said.

"Yes, I've lived life, enough." Lester said.

"One, sometimes can't." Italiano said. "By the time you turn in all paper work, your victim has been raped again, someone has been shot dead."

"Italiano, I can't be in agreement with you, about that one." Lester said.

"You're not in agreement with me, about many things. But you've seen me run from danger, and survive." Italiano said. "Only reason, Reymundo survived, is because of his game with

his brother, about each other being guilty about that gun for me? Turns out, Cobra, never did tell his own story. With Cobra gone, Astrid may now, talk."

Later that day in the room Gene is kept...

"I've taken you, Gene away." Wolf said. "We'll ask for that money. But first, I'd like you to learn how to keep a secret?"

"Wolf, you're scaring me now?" Gene said. "You should step away from me. My men, and I don't play."

"What I mean, I've heard they all left you to yourself? Is it they given up on the gang?" Wolf said. "You'll want to join us, after this, we'll be something?"

"Wolf, I'll scream!" Gene yelled.

"What is going on, Dragon? I thought you one of my men, why you've escaped jail?" Italiano asked. "We agreed, we don't hurt girls?"

"You agreed, you don't hurt girls. But call this, personal, Italiano?" Wolf said. "Gene, has agreed with me, we'll call it love. She'll join our gang."

"Ah--" Gene with cry tried to say something.

"Not sure, you know what gang I belong to, Wolf." Italiano warned.

"A detective, plan gone all wrong, with your joining in for the money?" Wolf proved he knew.

"We supposed to take the money, let the girl go. Now it's looking obvious, you're keeping her?" Italiano recriminated.

"Why don't you allow Gene talk, she can talk for herself? Gene?" Wolf asked still next to her.

"I, uhm?" Gene tried to say.

"Wolf, no more warning for some crimes." Italiano shot Dragon.

"Ah?" Dragon fell to the floor.

"How will we explain this to the cops. There is no paperwork that will explain this one?" Jimmy front of Italiano cried.

"Jimmy, I'm afraid, cops are wrong about me. Some paperwork, I don't turn in." Italiano walked out to his office in the abandoned company.

"Knew, I wasn't cop anymore? Not exactly cops, anymore?" Jimmy looked at Eren.

"Nope don't think, cops will consider us, cops, either. We might want to tell the truth about this body?" Eren asked.

"We know nothing about it?" Jimmy and Eren said.

"You know, now we're in trouble with the law, and Italiano." Eren said.

"You can't say, Italiano acted illegal? I mean not entirely. Dragon would have kept going with his crime, without allowing us, in. And if that'd happened, we'd never save a girl?" Jimmy said. "I'd say, that's a fair shot?"

"Kill?" Eren looked at the dead body on the floor. "I'm out!" Eren turned and hurried to the door.

"I, can't." Jimmy said. "I know too much. Afraid, Italiano will kill me, for knowing too much?"

"You know, Italiano would never kill, innocent!" Eren walked back to Jimmy.

"Exactly." Jimmy proved a point.

"Ah?" Eren and Jimmy looked at each other.

"Oh, my god!" Ezra walked in an office room. *"Which one of you done it?"*

"It wasn't me!" They both pointed to himself.

"I'm calling it out. Italiano!" Ezra walked to him. *"Don't know what happened, but it didn't happen on my watch! Not going down for it, man? Jimmy, Eren, your cops. Who you, Italiano, say, aren't cops? We should watch out, front of them—"* He pointed to them.

"They'll tell on us." Italiano knew his words. *"Hm?"* He looked at his men.

"Hm?" Jimmy and Eren walked to them.

"Yeah. Those men, have just shot Wolf down. Not saying, Wolf could keep his belt tight on?" Ezra said. *"He still a dead body."*

"Ah?" They all looked at Ezra.

"Was is it, Gene, cause he said, he had a thing for her. But, she having a thing for him, na?" Ezra said.

Hm?" They all looked at him.

"What, you don't believe me? Wolf said, no one would believe me. He'd tell Gene, to admit, it was just a date, all gone wrong?" Ezra sighed despair. *"I'm still telling on them, cause I need the cops on my side, for once. They'll forgive, my escape? You know, we all the same?"*

"It's all right, Ezra. No one here, knows anything about it." Italiano said.

"Cause they your men?" Ezra cried. "Not unless, I really need to watch out for you, Italiano?"

"Hm?" Italiano worried he'd been found out, working outside the law.

"Haha. I'm just kidding, man." Ezra hit his arm. "Relax, know you a real man of law."

"Haha." They all laughed.

"One too many bodies, under your watch, Italiano?" Ace asked helping one of his men out with the body.

"Hm?" Italiano looked at Jimmy and Eren.

"Hm?" Jimmy and Eren looked at each other.

"Ah?" Ezra questioned himself about them. "You aren't all thinking it, was me? Cause, it wasn't?"

"I walked in there, before you did. Was a body on the floor already." Italiano said.

"Afraid, you wouldn't believe me. You know, your men pointing the finger at me?" Ezra watched them.

"Haha?" They laughed.

"How will we get Ace to sell us any?" Italiano asked.

"Not, making any transaction with you, man." Ezra said. "Ace, and I got our own business, without you. With a body, not knowing who it was? You not caring a thing, to turn us in for it?"

"Cause, I don't know who it was. Cops will still find out, about that body? Just, can't waist time implicating myself, with

it, when I know nothing about it. Trying to make myself believe,
with you?" Italiano said.

"Yeah, like I said, you can't be trusted. You just asked
your men, to make sure the cops, find that body." Ezra said.
"Could be in. But only, you could really be the kill? Now, why?"

"Hm?" Italiano didn't deny it.

"Yeah, I could never know, right. Cause, that body would
just prove you are criminal, but work the same for cops, knowing
you'd never?" Ezra said.

"I'm telling you something, Ezra. If I see something I
don't like, when you know, I don't kill? Anyone gives me a
reason to pull that trigger, I will." Italiano said.

"Ooh!" Ezra moved back as though spooked.

"Guy, why don't I solve your problem, instead of giving
you anymore?" Gene had walked out the room.

"What is it, Gene. We've gotten paid, you'll be out there
soon." Italiano said.

"I'll call, tell them it's been a mistake. Work for you?"
Gene said. "We all know, here, think Wolf did, who I am?" Gene
said.

"Who, are you, Gene?" Italiano must ask.

"Well, for one, done bank robbery?" Gene said. "Unless
you're a real cop, you'll deny me a gansta, work for you?"

"Hm?" Italiano looked at her. "Your father has paid you
out, Gene. What you do after you've been left front of your
home, is your problem?"

"Italiano?" Gene asked.

"Gene, I have enough trouble, as you've said." Italiano said. "Guys, why don't you take her home?"

"Let's go, Gene. Let's just hope they believe, an old badge." Jimmy took her arm.

"All right, Italiano?" Gene looked at him. "Thank, you." She walked away with Jimmy.

"What she thanking you for? Yeah, man, what she mean by all that?" Ezra asked. "You'll tell me, cop Eren, still a cop, aren't you?" He looked at Eren.

"Hm? Would," Eren looked at Italiano. "except I don't know none."

"Why let Gene go, you know we could use a girl like that?" Ezra asked. "Boy, you don't make no sense, even if you were gangsta?"

Gene is home…

"You real quiet girl. A man was just killed front of you?" Jimmy stopped front of Gene's home in a cop car.

"Yeah, he almost did me like Mona." Gene got off the car and shut the door behind her.

"Ah, all right." Jimmy drove away.

"Hm?" Gene watched a cop car drive away.

"Baby!" Gene's mother ran out to her with hug and cry.

"Mom, missed you too." Gene also hugged her. "You won't believe it, but I hardly felt them enemy?"

"Hm?" Gene's mom smiled. "Dad, paid just enough money for it, dear." She hugged her inside the house.

"Gene, what trouble do you get yourself into? I'm not bailing you out, again?" Dad was in the living room.

"Hm? Missed you too, Dad." Gene walked to her room.

"You know, she loves you, too." Gene's mom said in the living room.

Jimmy is back...

"Guys, mission complete." Jimmy said.

"It's just Ezra can believe what a good guy you are, would never kill anyone." Ace continued an ongoing conversation with guys. *"But, I will not trust you, Italiano."*

"You don't have to trust me. Just do business with me." Italiano said.

"I'm turning you into cops. Your men never would. Probably had a reason for it, the why. But it was still a kill, you didn't turn in." Ace said. *"Not convinced you're not a cop. We all in trouble with that one. Believed one."*

"Ace," Italiano turned on a cigar. *"you be careful with that one. You turn me in? Your word, against, mine."*

"He still a cop." Jimmy said.

"I got that one." Ace said.

"So, we all in?" Eren cried.

"Wasn't you, Eren, who took care of that body?" Italiano was front of him as though asking for a confession.

"No!" Eren assured front of Ace.

"Then, you have nothing to worry about." Italiano assured. *"Ace, ready to do business?"*

"Not, with you man." Ace hurried out his office.

"Hm." Italiano looked at his men. *"I'm out to my office."*

"Sure thing, man." Eren watched him walk out the office.

"Relax, man." Jimmy asked.

"You probably knew what you were getting yourself into, when you joined, Italian mafia, but, I had no idea?" Eren said.

"Didn't." Jimmy said. *"But after the guys lied about my name tag, there was no explanation I could give them. No way I wasn't losing my badge, then."*

"So, you stay quiet about it. Till they catch you?" Eren said.

"Suppose, they never do." Jimmy was front of Eren. *"Mona knows nothing? Kept here?"*

"Na, man you guys can't drag me into this? But you have." Eren looked to a side at the floor.

"So, Italiano has set Gene free, isn't it?" Ezra was in Italiano's office.

"Has." Jimmy said.

"He, didn't, want anyone coming, asking, any, questions." Eren made sure to explain?

"Haha." They laughed about a plan gone wrong.

"Italian Briefcase, is it, he's at?" Ezra is in an abandoned building. *"You know the economy hasn't been working itself*

enough, when you got a place to play in?" He looked around an abandoned company.

"Haha?" They laughed.

"Yeah, they need some professional, least serious about economics?" Ezra said. "Cause, Art, ain't doing it."

"Haha." They laughed.

Days Later. Art is in Mona's office...

"Working those numbers. Isn't the easiest, when you go below and above zero, like some game?" Art walked in the office.

"Just want your best, Art. Mr. McDudley can do the rest." Mona said.

"Haha." They laughed.

"Needing stability." Art smiled. "Working on it, for my group."

"What group is that?" Mona asked. "Made of who?"

"Stolen clients." Art said.

"Haha." They laughed.

"Mona, Wolf has appeared dead on some sidewalk." Italiano walked in the office.

"Can't say I'm not sorry?" Mona said.

"Mona, the man raped you?" Italiano said. "You could lie for whatever reason, but Wolf wanted credit for his crime? He boasted about it?"

"Italiano, I've learned to say the word rape. Still can't tell enough, what that means." Mona cried.

"You know, I would have done anything to save you from it?" Italiano said. "I go undercover for many things, but I'd kill the moment—" Italiano said.

"Italiano, we're not a gun?" Mona said.

"Not sure, a man knows a gun, when he dare—" Italiano said.

"Italiano, I'm okay now." Mona smiled. "Italiano, you're still with us, right? I mean money hasn't given you reason to join the wrong team?"

"Still part of Detective's P I." Italiano said.

"Italiano, before Detective's P I, what division were you?" Mona asked.

"I must get back to an office, Mona." Italiano said. "Just thought you might like to know, Wolf isn't part of this world anymore."

"Thank you. One less worry." Mona watched him walk out the door. "Who was it?"

"Wolf had many enemies, Mona. Think we're clear on that one?" Italiano continued to the door.

"Italiano, some reason to fly out here?" Art asked.

"Nice to see you, friend?" Italiano walked out the door.

"Friend." Art smiled. "He looks so much like his brother. But I'm sure, not any like him." Art said.

"Will we continue a conversation in person?" Mona asked.

"Think we might like to forget the hotel business for a couple days?" Art said.

"Art, know, I'd never do anything like that." Mona smiled.

"Mona, think about it? Numbers all day? You like to tell a story. And you tell it well. People enjoy a good story." Art insisted.

"Is this about you, Art?" Mona asked. *"Because, I have no need—"*

"For a say?" Art asked.

"Oh, no." Mona put a folder on other folders. *"I have lots say. I just don't think anyone would care for it?"*

"We, do." Art assured on the other side of her desk. *"A bit afraid, what big mouth Mona will say. Only, someday, you know we might appreciate?"*

"I'd like to see that." Mona was front of him.

"Why did you leave, Guy's world?" Art asked.

"Guy was busy signing everything into contract, while I worked with Lance Scavo. Soon as it became Guy's world, I had nothing more to do there." Mona said.

"Mona, while you worked for Lance, found out, there's no Mr. in that one? Did you cheat on me?" Art asked front of her.

"Art?" Mona looked at him without smile. *"I never did."*

"Whoo!" Art smiled. *"I thought maybe, Lance had taken advantage of us guys not being present?"* Art said.

"Because, I was never your girl." Mona said. "My private life, like yours is private."

"My life, is all over the newspaper?" Art said.

"I'd like to have found out, it was just story." Mona said. "Be sure, all those years, I cried for you, you were faithful to me."

"Guy?" Art asked. "Is, who you talk about all the time. I'm like, just a bounce off?"

"Haha." Mona laughed. "Let's not forget, time has progressed, and life has brought us, to this moment. You're both a family man."

"But you, Mona, continue to be single." Art pointed out. "I don't think you're—"

"Who cares." Mona said.

"I, do." Art held her hand. "I want you to be happy, someday. I am." He let her hand go. "I've understood, just like I want to be happy, you do too."

"I always thought, a bit selfish. You know," Mona walked away. "to move on with your life without me? Then, I threw my diary. Knew there was no reason anymore, keep it. My best friend hadn't called back."

"Could have told me, you went along be happy with that girl from that restaurant. You never did notice, but you went on talking like no one was front of you, when we went to that cabin, had dinner?" Mona said. "You know, the other times, you cooked breakfast, lunch for us. You loved, your cooking. Haha. Talk about kiss, that chef." Mona laughed.

"Mona, you laugh too much. Nothing that lasted. Someday, one might believe your laughs?" Art was front of her.

"One, might?" Mona said with nod. *"Now, you remember you're a married man. Know how much I hate you belong to another. But I hate it even more, you make another cry, not because of me?"*

"Haha." Art laughed. *"All right, so we'll be professional continue that talk about a company with business meetings. Know I can't live outside a meeting room? A tell about, numbers? Present time. We must all be, part of? Can't stress that enough."*

"Love your human, Art. I've heard, you were a number expert, at Garrett's?" Mona smiled. *"Then, you were novel, at Four Seasons of Memories. But this is all I have to offer, Art. I'm sorry."* She walked to her desk.

"Mona, come on?" Art asked. *"You know there are things, need be said. No one else willing to talk about? Not, like you."*

"Guy, and I have pushed you enough to make you say them?" Mona smiled. *"So, why don't you be honest, and leave this place? Get back to Four Seasons of Memories, have your talk. Peace talks, that is? I'll be all right at Blue Bay City."*

"Mona, I have a feeling this was supposed to happen just the way it did. We supposed to have a say. Least we can do, you know, so Mr. McDudley will do his work?" Art said.

"Mr. McDudley became our president, because he knew what he was doing." Mona said. *"I'm sure, he needs no one to walk behind him at every turn, asking him to do."*

"We all could use a bit of help. Besides, this world was built by its people?" Art said. *"Shouldn't we have a say? You go out into this world lots. People always have a say. I think they*

trust you, to their ideas. Then, you may write your conclusion on paper?"

"Is that, what you think I do?" Mona walked over to him. "Steal your ideas? I mean in another words, still adds up to steal? Accusing me, Art? As if, I had no say?"

"Haha." They laughed.

"Let's put it this way, Mona?" Art asked. "Front of a same world we know, it's just you and I. Guilty." Art with whisper accused.

"Ha?" They both laughed.

"I'm not promising you anything." Mona walked front of a window in her office. "With false accusations against me, I might as well prove myself innocent. I see no better way, than at a business meeting. People see a full picture then. Well, not the world. Enough people."

"Mona, I know you'll get yourself out your comfort zone. Create that world of books." Art said.

"Art, why when you may own your say, are you willing to work for me?" Mona asked.

"Can't work for Guy." Art said.

"Haha." They laughed.

"Why not, you're best friends? When I thought, I was the one that brought you guys apart, with my falling in love with my best friend, turns out, my best friend was a known traitor, to many." Mona said.

"Hoits." Art held his heart. "Mona, I think you've heard this one. Only thing I know, is, I rule the world." He smiled.

"Lance Scavo." Mona did recognize. "Enough people heard it."

"Haha." They laughed.

"Mona, as the friends, we should have been. You know, with a continuation of your diary? Did Lance and you fall in love? I'd have understood. Guy and I were out your life. Were." Art turned without looking away.

"Ha?" Mona laughed.

"Desmon having married you, had left his heart involved with a past. Loretta." Art said.

"I Mona, Art, was the only who made such mistake. Haha. I mean throughout my life, seeing myself alone in that picture of my life, made lots." Mona admitted. "One day I woke up from my fantasy world and, said, I'm too good for dreams."

"Haha." They laughed.

"You'd like to think, mistake was your own. Forgive Desmon lot's better." Art knew.

"No, forget Desmon and I once, were an item." Mona said.

"Must, now. He's engaged his heart." Art said.

"Just hoping there's someone out there, Art, for me?" Mona looked at him.

"I hope so, too." Art said. "I mean because I'm a married—"

"Your heart has been committed." Mona smiled.

Blue Bay Hotel. Meeting about Mona's company, Create World…

"Sometimes, we have to start all over, only from where we've left off." Art said front of a meeting room. "Such is, Mona's business, here at Blue Bay City. The economy has rolled us here, and so we move forward from here. Making sure, all is calculated, to fit, well an existing economy. We'd like everyone to have a chance, at the life. Mona offers, to every kind of person. Like a personal experience. What we try giving." Art said next to a board. "As you can see numbers can't be matched to Four Seasons of Memories, we all know why. Guy is a businessman, and it shows. Mona, have I been mistaken, may we match numbers, to Guy's business at his meetings?"

"Haha. Art, why I've hired an expert." Mona said. "Be sure, if we may, someday match numbers to now Guy's Four Seasons of Memories, being his own company, we'll in fact, do that." Mona turned to look at everyone in the meeting room. "Of course, with a difference. Haha. We won't cheat you out, finest from A to Z."

"Haha." Everyone laughed.

"Because, some in economy have stepped forward, because we can't allow, we be stepped back." Art smiled front of a meeting room.

"Ha. Hope, Guy, doesn't find out about that one, he'll only continue on matching our performance. Some people, we can't catch up to." Art did laugh.

"Haha?" Everyone laughed.

"Maybe, we haven't talked to Lance, knows not impossible." Dario walked in a meeting room.

"We all know, who Guy is." Liam smiled in a meeting room. "But, we also know, who Mona has been?" He looked at everyone for agreement.

"Haha." Everyone applauded for their boss Mona.

"Thank you." Mona stood up from her seat and walked front of a meeting room. "Nice how you create a meeting room. Always expect to walk in, as if in a different meeting room, Art."

"Thank you, Mona." Art is next to her. "Can't do it, without your personnel."

"We can't." Mona smiled at the people behind a meeting next to a table with folders, pencils, handbooks.

"Looks like you've covered business economy, today?" Liam said.

"Liam, one we like to be attended by, for a meal." Mona smiled. "And like Liam, there are many of you, all the way to an office. I call these meetings, allow us all to know, a hotel to be run to what it has become, takes more than me." Mona said.

"Haha." Everyone laughed.

"Today, it's a year this company welcomed meetings, by Art. Why I've invited you all." Mona smiled at a meeting. "This meeting, I'd like to thank you for your excellent work. I'd also like to thank Art, for his idea, of opening up my own world of writing." Mona said.

"Haha." Everyone applauded.

"Thank you, Mona." Art was at the right end side of a meeting table.

"Well, if we may now enjoy lunch?" Mona had a set meeting room with foods. "Of course, you all get back to your everyday office, work place, while Art and I remain in our own, at Blue Bay Hotel."

"Ha." Everyone thanked with applaud.

"You may enjoy your day, with lunch." Mona said. "Art and I, invite you to walk the hotel, there is more going on than a hotel room."

"Haha." Everyone laughed.

"There is." Art smiled.

"Starting with a swimming pool." Somra at the door smiled.

"Haha." Everyone walked to enjoy foods served front of a meeting room.

"Create World, will it remain that?" Liam asked.

"Mona hasn't said anything." One of the writers smiled.

"Liam, have you a new best friend?" Mia asked.

"Oh, never, that might hurt me more?" Liam said.

"Haha." Liam and Mia laughed.

"So many questions, Mona. Will you keep the name, Create World? Is it competition against your own…Guy?" Mia asked.

"Haha." Mona laughed. "Can't really call it competition when we're owned by, boss Guy. Ooh, that hurts. You know, because I'm used to owning myself." Mona walked with a plate of food to a table.

"So, bosses table." Art sat next to her at a table in a meeting room.

"Yeah, only way I make you listen to any ideas I have. You know, I've painted myself in your world?" Mona laughed.

"Haha." Art and Mona laughed.

"They are too close. Guy won't like this, one?" Dario had a tray with a napkin on it.

"Guy never likes anything that's going on here, since Art became a new haunt." Somra said.

"How, will we do this?" Dario said.

"Do, what?" Somra said. "It's Mona's world. When one can own, their say."

"Their, do?" Dario did question. "When love, involved."

"You really believe, in love?" Somra asked.

"Is it personal, you speak?" Dario asked. "Somra, you answer to Mona, forget we are owned by one more, boss?"

"Hm?" Somra looked at him. "Even if that was way things are? You tell me, what could I possibly do about it?"

"Maybe, you're right?" Dario walked to Mona's table. "Art, must we get paid to do this all day?"

"Do, what?" Art asked.

"I'll clear this table." Dario took a glass from the table.

"Thank you." Art smiled.

"Mona, will you be joining Create World, this week?" Dario cleared her plate.

"I'll be enjoying weekend cruise." Mona said.

"It's her new religion." Art watched Dario walk away with a tray.

"Art, I might believe your jealous?" Mona smiled.

"It's what I was hoping for." Art said.

"Haha. You like, Desmon don't expect me to stay single?" Mona asked.

"Hm?" Art looked at Mona. "We've been through this before?"

"Well, you're not always convincing, wanting me to be happy with another?" Mona said.

"Ah, but would you?" Art asked. "All past, has come flushing back to you, between you and I? Before Greg walked in the picture? You know, video meetings. Still present in one same meeting?"

"Ah, funny?" Mona said. "Haha. How could I have forgotten that? Maybe, because Greg was real? You know a real phone call. Never forgot for a second to at least text me?"

"Hm, so that's how it's done? You know, I thought—" Art looked at everyone watching and listening in. "Is, what real meetings, do?"

"Well, don't stop now? I'm believing every word?" Mona asked.

"Haha." They both laughed.

"I thought people in love, phone call, no phone call? Never forgot each other." Art said.

"You're talking friendship, Art?" Dario asked. "Because, I can relate," Dario played with a napkin on the tray he held. "Mona?"

"Haha?" Everyone laughed.

"Video call with Guy, all different. You know, business." Dario smiled.

"Darius, must you?" Art got up from a table. "My office waiting."

"Dario, have you forgotten who's boss, with contract signed?" Mona asked.

"You'll thank me someday." Dario said.

"Haha. Not today." Mona walked out a meeting room.

"Was real conversation." Dario did apologize to a table.

"Hm, ah?" They mumbled out a meeting room.

"When, one has more than one boss?" Dario held a tray up in hand.

Four Seasons of Memories...

"Thought maybe you and Darla would enjoy office chats. Fall in love again someday. She's left your office alone. And we continue to be married." Magda said.

"Magda, will you stop talking Darla. Once was her world." Guy said.

"I believe, it's still her world. There isn't anyone who doesn't know her, and outside this office. I doubt, it wasn't Mr. Scavo who did that for her." Magda said.

"Mr. Scavo did lots of good things. Only, all that once his, is mine." Guy said. "You, have an idea, of all that it takes, to make such transfer? Just anyone, takes lots—"

"Someone once said, 'Boss, I came to this office, with more than your ideas.'" Magda smiled.

"You've quoted Art." Guy said. *"Words that explain me as well."*

"We love to quote Art." Magda smiled. *"Once, your best friend."* She did remind. *"To take over, an empire. Yes, love all you are, Guy."* She kissed him. *"Should I call a meeting?"*

"No." Guy said. *"You allow them to have their own meetings. I see no reason for us to involve ourselves."*

"Very well." Magda said. *"I'll return to my office. Because of Darla? What is happening with our relationship. We might want to talk about it, before we fight about it?"*

"Magda, we've been through enough, to allow our relationship end, like this?" Guy reminded.

"It's what I've told myself all this time. On that cruise, you were reunited with them, Guy, might have been life who brought you back together. Way life is. Then again, your begin of signing everyone into contract, must it have had an end, with Four Seasons Of Memories?"

"Ah?" Guy was he caught, in love? *"It was family who brought me back, here, continues to bring me back."*

"Aah?" Magda with nod of her head understood?

"I had remembered all." Guy said.

"Guy, it was you who insisted, I didn't talk about your life?" Magda said.

"I insisted on not finding out who I was, when forgotten all. I just wanted to continue our love together. Especially after finding out the kids weren't mine."

"I thought, you'd want to find that out, before anything else?" Magda said. "I was wrong. You love those kids, just as if they were your own."

"Magda, you forget Desmon." Guy said.

"Desmon? Mona with her silence, tells lots." Magda said. "Forget us, Guy? You have every right to. Only did, what you asked. Quiet about your life."

"Magda?" Guy held her hand. "Happened just the same, I someday, remembered it all. Just knew, if I didn't remember it on my own, I'd be a complete stranger to their life? Don't punish yourself for it, not when it was my decision to continue without knowing my own life."

"Ah?" Magda looked at him. "I suppose I knew once you remembered all, our live together wouldn't be, the same?"

"Not your fault, Magda." Guy hugged her from behind.

"Guy, if you ever have a chance to your family life, I'll remember my life, single." Magda turned around and looked in his eyes.

Guy son and Art son are in the office...

"A new life from what your dad would have offered us." Sage smiled in her husband's office.

"You continue to be an actress." Guy said.

"Guy, will you forgive my career?" Sage kissed him.

"Someone has to take care of our son and daughter?" Guy smiled.

"You're right. I'll get back to family." Sage walked out the office.

"Grandma Sherese, you've got Great-grandkids now." Guy smiled. "Hope you know that?"

"Haha? Why wouldn't grandma Sherese not know that?" Art walked in the office. "Just saw Sage walk out this office."

"You haven't been talking to the secretary?" Guy asked. "You know, we have history together? When the wife, is too busy, with family."

"Nina. Uhm, no, we don't talk." Art said. "Ever."

"Why all the visits to grandma Imelda? You want to let her find out, with it all, she's grandma?" Guy asked.

"Ah, no." Art looked to an office window. "Just, uhm, like the woman."

"Blood calls." Guy smiled. "I've heard, the secretary goes there visit, lots?"

"Yeah, they met once. Talk lots?" Art said.

"Well," Guy looked from an open folder as he stood front of a desk. "don't go joining conversation?" He closed a folder.

"Of, course, not?" Art said. "It's, uhm, family, Guy. Sister Bethany, grandma Imelda?"

"Oh, Art, will you stop apologizing? Haven't we heard the story already?" Guy asked.

"Yeah, but this is us. Kids now?" Art said.

"Now, we have kids." Guy said. "Well, I do. When will you catch up to me? You know, your kids will someday be jealous, they're not the older ones?"

"Why, would they get jealous?" Art asked.

"Older ones have been round longer. We, uhm, get to have more responsibility." Guy said.

"What makes you the older of us, bro?" Art asked.

"Am I not?" Guy asked.

"Yeah, sure. But this doesn't go the same, for our kids?" Art said.

"Soon, as you hurry up and have them." Guy had folders ready stacked.

"You, working on that already?" Art looked at stacked folders.

"What do you think? Call me the older one." Guy said.

"Thought someday, we'd be cops?" Art said.

"So, we thought." Guy said.

"Instead, we've built our own company." Art said.

"Family company, dad has refused to be part of. Married, to Magda. He's got his own world." Guy said. "Why blame him?"

"Magda, thought we might not welcome her, as mother." Art said. "I know she says, it's not the place she'd like to take. But would it be fair, we'd treat her like anyone else, in this company?"

"No, wouldn't." Guy is front of his desk.

"Guy, we will try to be better than last generation, as dad once said, 'Far as we know.' What if we fail? Marriages, business?" Art asked.

"We talk to Mona. Think she'll be reminder enough, how it's not fair, we steal from Lance again?" Art said.

"What was it, with Sage? I mean for Lance and Mona to get along badly like that? But Sage, is my girl. I'm not dad Guy?" Guy said.

"Think Lance knows that. You know, Lance might have made a mistake like that with Mona, but I think he can tell when he'd have crossed that line, with someone?" Art said.

"Sage is an actress, is what grandma Sherese says." Guy said.

"That's a…for grandma Sherese to say." Art smiled. "Why don't we get back to work? You know, we can't allow Art finish our numeric. So why don't we get started on that one? An investment today, a fruitful tree for tomorrow?"

"Ha. Ha?" Guy pointed at his brother. "You're good, like that."

"Thanks." Art said. "Why you have me working here." He walked out the office.

"Art." Sage walked in the office as Art walked out.

"Sage." Art continued on his way to his office.

"You talked about me?" Sage asked Guy.

"We, might have mentioned you." Guy smiled. "How was that meeting, with Mr. Scavo? I still find it hard to understand, that closeness between, you two?"

"I'm not Nina, Guy." Sage kissed her husband.

"Must we?" Guy put his hand over his head. "Talk Nina?"

"Ah?" Sage asked. "I'm sure, I've chosen you?"

"Let's have lunch." Guy smiled. "Must you be funny like that?"

"Funny, isn't what I'm trying to be." Sage walked down hallways with her husband.

"Know it." Guy smiled.

"So, you pretend you're my girl, everything will be all right?" Lance said over the phone. "As your boyfriend, I say you forget anything that has to do with Guy."

"Lance, I'm not Mona." Nina said over the phone. "Anything that has to do with Guy and I, might like to forget it? I'm not dating you for any reason."

"Nina, it's not like that, will you just please listen to Mona, when she talks about us, a couple?" Lance asked. "We break up every time. What you should be doing every time you cross paths with, that Guy guy. Believe me, I've known his father all these years?"

"Lance, Guy is front of me. Son Guy." Nina said.

"Sorry, Nina, I completely ignored you. You might understand by now, Guy is my husband? Not only is there a ring on to our love, we have two adorable children?" Sage said.

"Of course." Nina said.

"Nina, are you still on the phone?" Guy asked.

"No." Nina hung up the phone. "Boss, you need anything else?"

"I'm going out for lunch with my wife, Sage." Guy said. "Have Lance and you talked date?"

"No." Nina said.

"Then you're still in time to hang up the phone, give him not another chance to word you into that romance." Guy said.

"Boss, your wife is right front of you. I don't think that should concern—" Nina said.

"Oh, Nina, I agree with my husband. Lance? Someone your own age would take, you serious?" Sage said.

"Hm?" Nina looked at Sage. "Boss, have a great lunch, with your wife."

"Hm?" Guy looked at Sage. "May I remind, Dario?"

"Dario, is nothing but work." Sage cried. "I'll leave you to your jealous." She walked to an elevator room.

"Nina, you talking with Lance every chance you get, doesn't look good for this company?" Guy said at the other side of Nina's desk.

"Lance is nothing but business. So, we don't all agree with his business?" Nina said.

"Nina, someday we forgave you walked in our home, lied about grandpa Corbin, gave you a job? Must we regret—" Guy asked.

"Guy?" Art walked to them. "Still around."

"Ah?" Guy turned to look at him.

"Sage still around, is waiting for me." Guy hurried to the elevator room.

"I have no idea why I continue to work here. He's right, why am I trusted any?" Nina said.

"Because, you're a different girl, now, Nina." Art said.

"Art, you knew me when I wasn't a good little girl. And, now you're the only that continues to trust me? See how in my life, I've changed, why?" Nina said.

"Why?" Art asked.

"Hm?" Nina looked at her desk.

"Nina, is it you don't want to answer, because it's for my brother, Guy?" Art asked.

"Someday, I worked at a desk that was bad business. Guy changed that desk, entire office for me?" Nina said.

"I'd like to think, I had something to do with it?" Art said.

"Ha?" They laughed.

"See, you at Imelda's?" Art whispered.

"Art?" Nina whispered. "They'll find us out?" She cried.

"See, you!" He whispered with demand.

"Okay." She whispered.

Imelda's home...

"Nina, it's always nice to see you. Just have to hide everything?" Imelda said.

"Ah?" Nina looked at her.

"Forgive Imelda, she likes to be funny." Art said.

"That includes my grandson, Nina." Imelda whispered.

"Ah?" Nina looked at Imelda.

"What did she tell you, Nina?" Art hurried to ask. *"Grandma, Imelda, what did you tell Nina?"*

"Imelda, you should know something about your grandkids?" Nina said.

"No, don't—" Art nodded.

"What's that?" Imelda, asked.

"Guy and I—" Nina said.

"I've stolen, Nina's heart." Art hurried to tell. *"It's all you know, Imelda?"* Art looked at Nina. *"Na?"* He nodded.

"Hm?" Imelda with hands on waist looked at Art. *"So, it's you at fault?"*

"Haha?" Imelda and Art laughed.

"Ah?" Nina looked at them.

"Oh, Nina, it's okay. So, you've stolen my son Art's heart. He's, single?" She whispered to her.

"Haha." They laughed.

"Ah?" Nina looked at Art.

"Brother, thought I'd find you here?" Guy walked in the kitchen where food is being prepared.

"Guy?" Art walked to the table in the dining room. *"Just doing some homework?"*

"Imelda, Nina." Guy kissed Imelda hello.

"I remember once, you kissed Nina, hello too?" Imelda asked.

"Guy, Art, how are you!" Bethany walked in the kitchen with hug for both.

"Aren't you going to say hi to Nina?" Imelda asked her granddaughter.

"Nina, how are you." Bethany asked. "Don't mind me, I'll be doing homework just the same in the living room."

"All right." They all said.

"So, you'll be doing homework some?" Guy walked to his brother in the dining room. "Why, are you always here? Know grandma Sherese will feel bad, you pretending anyone else is, grandma. Wouldn't want, Imelda to find out?"

"Find out, what, guys?" Imelda walked in the dining room. "Lately, seems like you all have secrets, from me?"

"Ah?" They both looked at each other.

"Does Nina, have anything to do with any of this?" Imelda turned to look at Nina in the kitchen stirring food.

"I, what?" Nina walked in the dining room.

"Na, Nina, is actually what brings us together. You know, criminal she is?" Guy looked at her. "Kind of girl would steal, uhm, ah? Guy's heart." Guy looked at her.

"Yeah, a guy's heart." Imelda walked to the kitchen. "Can't wait to have great-grandchildren." She turned from the stove to them.

"Hm?" Guy bit his lip. "Now, what does Imelda know, that I've not told her, guys?"

"Ah?" Art and Nina looked at each other.

"Now, for that, two people have to have a serious relationship, leads to marriage?" Imelda smiled front of them. "Well, you're already married, Guy."

"Yeah, with two kids." Guy said. "So?"

"Oh, Nina and I can't wait to have our own kids, too, only we're too young to make a commitment like that." Art said. "Right Nina, someday, you will?"

"Ah?" Nina thought. "Yeah, you too, Art."

"Just ah, thought two of you were in love, already?" Bethany walked in the dining room.

"That food is almost ready." Imelda walked to the kitchen again.

"Why aren't you telling mom, Art?" Bethany asked.

"Cause, we—" Guy hurried to answer.

"Guy's, married already Bethany?" Art said.

"Ooh, Art, don't you try to be funny about what we all know, here?" Bethany asked Art.

"Bethany, mom Imelda might need our help?" Nina took her to the kitchen.

"Ah, had no idea Bethany, new anything that was going on in my life. I'm sure, Sage and I had invited her to that wedding?" Guy said.

"Ah? Maybe, we aren't that close of a family?" Art shrugged.

"I'll see you. I'm letting Bethany know—" Guy walked in the kitchen.

"That, Guy is already married, to Sage!" Art walked behind Guy in the kitchen.

"Do, we really have to act like twins?" Guy turned round front of Art.

"Ha?" Art brushed his hair back front of Guy.

"Guys, dinner?" Bethany asked.

"Yes, guys, you know you're like family, stay for dinner? You know, it's a family night?" Imelda asked.

"Ah?" Art and Guy looked at each other.

"Why does it seem, they got this whole thing, wrong?" Guy whispered to Art.

"What, is it they got wrong, am I not understanding anything?" Art asked.

"You know, very well what I mean. That kiss, meant nothing, you know, actress?" Guy said.

"Actress?" Art asked.

"Not, about Sage. Just Nina." Guy said.

"Guys?" Bethany was side middle of them.

"Love you, like sis." Guy smiled. "Especially when you got it all right."

"When don't I?" Bethany smiled.

"Ah?" Art looked at her. "Can we just forget this, and eat?"

"You must be hungry, Art." Bethany said.

"I'm sure, Sherese won't mind sharing grandkids. So, I'll only have to pull the phone from my ear, one more time?" Imelda said.

"Haha." They laughed.

"I'll help serve plates." Bethany said.

"Imelda, don't mind, I invite, Sage?" Guy asked.

"Of course not, we love Sage." Bethany said. "So, she isn't behind a screen anymore?"

"Haha?" They all laughed.

At a dinner table...

"Sage, thank you for coming. Guy would never stay for dinner, unless you were invited." Imelda put a last plate on the table.

"Why you've invited me?" Sage asked.

"Why you've accepted?" Imelda smiled.

"Ha. Missed this home. Always feels like family." Sage said.

"It is." Bethany said.

"You have no, idea, Bethany." Sage said.

"Ah?" Bethany looked at grandma Imelda.

"What?" Imelda asked.

"Sage, is this about Nina, because Nina and Art—" Bethany tried to say.

"I know, Bethany. It's the part you have no idea about, has me worried?" Sage said.

"What, are you talking about, Sage. You always say things, I don't understand. Would like to?" Bethany asked.

"Sage, only means, that we hang out as if we were real family, Bethany." Guy interrupted a conversation. *"You know, we could never understand somethings, why people are like real family—"*

"Being complete, strangers." Art also joined a conversation.

"There, we've understood it." Imelda said. *"I'll tell you, why? Like my own mother used to say, Mama fits everyone in her heart, as in her home."*

"Mama's words, nice." Sage smiled. *"I couldn't be any happier, invited anywhere else?"* She got a cup and looked at it. *"Ah?"* She drank.

"One day, you will bring my great grandchildren?" Imelda asked. *"I can't wait to meet them, what are they, nine and ten?"*

"Well, Art's still to begin on that one." Guy said.

"Haha." They laughed.

"Nice to see a table full with family." Angelo walked in the kitchen. *"I'm sorry, it was work this time."*

"It'd better been." Imelda got up for another plate.

"Haha." They laughed.

"Imelda still fighting her husband." Art laughed.

"Haha." They laughed.

"Way, we'll be." Sage said.

"Haha." They laughed.

"So, Guys, it's a full table, when you're not here. When, will you bring the kids?" Angelo asked.

"Ah?" Art looked at Sage.

"Soon, as Sherese understands, Corbin and her aren't the only great-grands?" Sage said.

"Haha." They laughed.

"Here, you are sweetheart." Imelda put Angelo's plate front of him.

"Thank you, Imelda." Angelo said. "Love end of the day. A served hot plate of food."

"Haha." They laughed.

"You will forgive us, but our kids wait." Guy said at the dining room door.

"Yes, do continue dinner uninterrupted." Sage said.

"Oh, don't be silly, Sage, we're done eating." Imelda walked them to the door.

"And, we can continue talking built, in the living room?" Art told Nina as they walked to the dining room hallway.

"Art, what should I tell grandma Sherese?" Guy walked back in the dining room.

"I'll be home later?" Art looked at Bethany who was behind him.

"Yeah, Art and I, we still have a last argument?" Bethany smiled at Guy.

"Nina, you need a ride?" Guy asked.

"Don't want any trouble, with Sage?" Nina said.

"Ah, don't be silly, Guy, any of us can take her home?" Bethany said.

"All right, then without worries, I'm headed home." Guy walked to meet with Sage at the door. "All ready, Sage." He and she walked out the door.

Inside the home...

"Maybe, I should go home?" Nina said.

"Nina, you can't think you'll be faithful to Guy? For that, you'd have to interrupt, a married couple's date?" Art said.

"Hm?" Nina looked at Art.

"I'm sorry, Nina. I didn't mean that?" Art apologized. "Guy since friends, has given you all the time in the world? Because, you're friends?"

"Art, a minute in the dining room?" Bethany asked. "Sorry, Nina, mom has something to talk to him about?"

"It's, all right?" Nina said.

"Go, ahead and wait for him in the living room." Bethany closed an entrance door.

"Okay." Nina walked to the living room.

"Art, is there something going on, I don't know about?" Bethany asked.

"Ah, why would you think that? Of course, not?" Art said.

"You've denied it, twice. So, I'm sure there is something going on. That, I, don't know about?" Bethany demanded to know.

"I'll, explain, Bethany?" Nina walked in the dining room. "Sorry, just walked in here to tell you, I was going home to work on that built, alone?"

"Oh, come on, Nina, you know I didn't mean it?" Art said.

"Art, may I?" Bethany asked. "Don't get into something, you'll be jealous all your life? Also, don't do what Guy is doing? Looks like he's cheating front of his wife, at every turn?"

"Ah?" Art tried to say something.

"Not," Bethany didn't allow Art say anything. "realizing he's hurting Sage's feelings. Ah, you two fell in love with the same girl, didn't you?"

"No, wasn't at all like that?" Art denied.

"Then, how is it? Because, I see no explanation for any of this. Nina? I thought you were a nice girl, but..." Bethany looked at her. "I trusted you into, our home?"

"Bethany?" Art demanded her attention. "I'd met Nina before any of this happened. So, we looked at each other, talked. Apparently, Nina has no idea anyone has fallen in love, the moment they stare into her eyes?"

"Art, he's still your brother." Bethany accepted no excuse.

"When, feeling already exist. Didn't expect you, anyone to understand me?" Art said.

"Did you understand, Nina said yes, to a question Guy had asked?" Bethany asked. "Why am I even talking about this?"

"Bethany, I'm sorry? Why, I didn't want to talk about it, in the first place. You'd never understand, yet, Guy would understand it, all too well?" Nina said. "Oh, I'm looking so bad, right now, aren't I?"

"Aha?" Bethany crossed hands.

"If it makes you feel any better, I, uhm, did fall in love with your brother that moment I saw him, too." Nina said.

"What?" Art asked.

"But, I had no idea, that guy in that white hat, and Art were the same person? And, so when I saw Art, and Guy walking in the house, together? I hardly realize, well, I'd already met, Art and fallen in love with him?"

"All right? What?" Art asked.

"Hm?" Nina looked at Art. "Guy, left with his friends. Summer vacations. I got jealous, every time. Broke up with him because of it. When Guy came back, a second time, Art and I thought he'd left with his girl friends? We had no idea, he'd come back?"

"Not that we were dating?" Art said.

"Weren't. Thought it was all said and done. But, now, I can't seem to, hurt, either one?" Nina looked at Art.

"Try?" Bethany said.

"Why?" Art looked at his sister.

"Because, both of you seem to be playing with a same girl's, heart?" Bethany asked.

"What, about my heart, have you stopped to think, I might be in love, just like Guy is in love, yes, with Sage? From the *moment, I met her? Not, this weird, thing everyone imagines?"* Art cried?

"Art?" Bethany looked at him. "Nina?" She sighed.

"Ha?" Nina cried.

"Just know the moment grandma Imelda finds out about this one?" Bethany thought. "She'll put her hand over her heart and say, "Ay, my corazon."

"Hm?" Art and Nina looked at each other.

"She does it, all the time. When something has gone wrong?" Bethany asked.

"Ay, my corazon?" Grandma Imelda with hand on her heart is in the dining room hallway.

"Nothing you've not gone through, before?" Bethany did say.

"Ah?" Art and Nina looked at each other.

"Think these family dinners, are over?" Bethany sighed.

"What's going on, Imelda?" Angelo hugged Imelda.

"Nothing?" Bethany, Art and Nina said.

"Hm?" Imelda nodded many times looking at Angelo with cry.

"Oh, brother." Angelo said.

"I know, that Art is visit, but must I remind who granddaughter is?" Bethany cried.

"Oh, we love you all the same?" Grandpa Angelo said.

"Haha?" They laughed.

Sage and Guy are home…

"I take it, Imelda and Angelo have no idea what's going on, under their nose?" Sage said in the living room.

"What is it, that's going on?" Guy asked Sage.

"Please, Guy, will you be honest to yourself, for once?" Sage asked. "Nina and Art have made their hiding home, at Imelda's and Angelo's home. You know, Sherese and Corbin, would never?"

"Never?" Guy asked.

"Allow, that kind of situation?" Sage said.

"I don't know what you're talking about. But whatever it is, you are, I'm sure it's nothing like that." Guy asked himself.

"Guy? How many times have I been wrong before?" Sage asked.

"Too many to count?" Guy said.

"Hate to think, you're trying to laugh, when it's really cry?" Sage said.

"This is just jealous about Nina?" Guy said.

"No, this is about saving the family, yours, Guy." Sage said. "Rather than, my heart." She took off earrings.

"When all I care about, is you." Guy hugged her from behind.

"Someday, if you have the chance to prove it, you will?" Sage turned around and looked up at him.

"What do you, mean by it?" Guy looked in the mirror front of them.

"Nothing. Pay no attention to anything I say." Sage smiled.

"I'll go put the kids to sleep." Guy walked out the room.

"Thanks." Sage said. "I'll read a book, for them."

In Brian and Madelyn's room...

"Want my own room someday?" Brian asked Guy his father.

"Soon." Guy sat on his daughter Maddy's bed.

"I'm not a kid anymore dad." Brian insisted.

"You and mom have lots in common, Maddy, only thing you and I have in common is that soccer ball." Guy said to his daughter.

"Just hope you heard a word I said." Brian insisted about his room.

"So, don't you let mom Sage question where that ball, will take you someday?" Guy smiled.

"What are you talking about, dad?" Maddy asked.

"Oh, good, you're still awake." Sage walked in their room. "Dad, and I were just talking, about that soccer ball? You might want to remember, the books, come first?"

"Oh, that's what you were talking about?" Maddy said.

"Mom, can I have my own room?" Brian asked his mom.

"If you forget that soccer ball, and that soccer suit, remember school priority?" Sage said.

"Oh, that's not a fair one, Sage, we've talked about this?" Guy said. "My kids, too?"

"It's their decision, not your life anymore. We, also talked about that one?" Sage said.

"Fighting to an agreement, again." Brian sighed. "Still getting my own room, right?" He sat up on his bed.

"Putting them to bed, is what we should be doing?" Sage said.

"All right, you just talk them out of it?" Guy walked out the room.

"Guys, what do you say? Prepare for the future, part of your community?" Sage asked.

"Hm?" The kids looked at each other.

"Coach, is also part of a community?" Brian said. "With that ball."

"And, that whistle." Sage smiled front of two beds.

"Ha?" The kids looked at each other.

"Like a coach, sometimes in life, you got to play, more than one roll. You know, mine isn't only mother." Sage smiled. "And yours, won't only be soccer player. Coach." She tapped Brian's nose.

"Haha." They laughed.

A game begins. A ball is kicked in a soccer field. A girl in a soccer suit blue with white kicks the ball to another girl. That little girl runs with it, kicking it from one side to another between her feet, kicking it to another girl. Girls and boys turn *around as the girl passes them, with trick, they watch her fool other kids like them, taking that ball, taking that ball, taking that ball, all the way, all the way, to a, goal!*

"Take it all the way, all the way, all the way!" A coach outside a white line runs with crowd of kids inside white lines. "All the way to a goal!"

"I did it!" Maddy turned around and yelled.

"You're the best!" They hugged her. "You scored another!"

"I did!" Maddy cried.

"Great sis, can't deny which of us is best?" Brian said.

"That's my girl." Guy watched a coach celebrate with the kids.

"Guy, missed it, again." Sage was next to him.

"You did. Maddy just scored." Guy said

"Again." Sage smiled. "I love she's one of the best, Guy. But I really would like to see her prove herself, outside this field."

"Thanks, mom." Maddy walked to them.

"So, you've found out, my sister scored, not I?" Brian said.

"Proud of you, kids." Sage hugged them. "I know, this sounded all wrong. But, really proud of you."

"We are too." Art walked to them.

"Never a dull moment with soccer, the game." Nina said. "You're beating them down, inside the field?"

"Haha." The kids laughed.

"She's so good with kids. Wonder if you'll still be, once you have your own, Nina?" Sage asked. "By the way thanks for showing up?"

"Ah?" Nina looked at Sage. "The boss invited us. Thought, his wife knew?"

"Nina, we're family. You're invited to every family event." Sage said.

"Hm." Guy smiled. "Family, Nina, just like Sage said."

"About, my kids?" Nina said. "You wait a bit, my own kids will tell you what an excellent mother I am," Nina hugged Guy's kids. "like your own."

"She's gonna be best mom." Brian said.

"Not like you." Maddy hugged her mom.

"Sage to be best mom, mother must never forget, there's kids around." Nina smiled.

"Thanks, Nina, for the advice." Sage said. "I'll keep it in mind, once your kids are born."

"Ah." Nina smiled. "Art, the game is over, we should go?"

"You, uhm, came to the game, together?" Sage asked. "Do you see, Guy, how your brother and the secretary, are so close? Isn't that against, any policy rule at the company? There must be?"

"Ah?" Nina looked at Sage. "Why must that be?"

"Oh, because, nothing else will keep you from family? I mean, real family?" Sage said. "No one is willing to tell you, so, I must?" She looked at Guy and Art. "Just another employee at the office.

"Mom Sage, you're not being like Grandma Sherese?" Brian asked. "Nina, just came to see our game? Watch my sister Maddy make another goal?"

"Ah?" Sage looked at her son. "I forget, my kids are old enough to understand what's going on. Do you, son?"

"Sage, let's not forget they are my kids, too?" Guy asked. "Family here?"

"Right, Guy." Sage said.

"We were out the office at the same time. Then, we had dinner at Imelda's. Thought we'd might as well, arrive together at the game?" Nina explained.

"I, was wrong?" Sage smiled at Guy. "Art, you must take Sage home?"

"Good night. Congratulations, little one." Art walked away with Nina.

"Look, at them? I'm sure the kids have no idea what's going on. What an example?" Sage watched her kids run around with the ball with practice.

"Let's, uhm, allow our kids, their own life?" Guy asked. "Like, our own?" He kissed her.

"Guy, I hate to be wrong." Sage said. "But I'd hate even more your feelings be hurt."

"I love you, Sage." Guy kissed her.

"Guy, tell me, I'm not wrong about you?" Sage kissed him.

"Oh, they're still in love?" Brian told his sister with hands up side of him.

"Haha." They laughed.

"Come on, let's go home kids. Tomorrow, we have another game!" Guy walked back to their car with his family. "And, you're not wrong about me, Sage." He drove away.

In a driveway...

"Well, back at Imelda's house, for your car." Art said to Nina. "Looking like, borrowed time?"

"Is." Nina said.

"Ah?" Art looked at her. "Ah, we should get out of here, before—"

"Before, what?" Nina at her car door hurried to asked trying to avoid something.

"I kiss you." Art kissed her cheek.

"Ah, right." Nina said. "Good night." She got in the car.

"Good night." Imelda waved from the porch.

"Good night, Imelda." Art waved still on the driveway. "Like she's trying to catch us?"

"Shut up, she'll believe it?" Nina whispered.

"Haha?" They laughed.

Sage and Guy are home...

"Will you reconsider, looking at the awards top of a chimney?" Guy asked.

"Maddy is really good." Sage looked at awards at the chimney. "What about life?"

"The soccer ball, is her world." Guy said. "That's her life. Don't you take that away from her."

"Guy?" Sage said. "Sometimes kicking a ball, into a goal, is just the beginning of a championship?"

"Ah?" Guy looked at her. "Sage, sometimes, you tire me. And, it's not soccer we're playing? Why don't you take a break someday, enjoy life?"

"I do that for you all the time." Sage smiled.

"So, we continue this talk about who our kids will grow up to be, another day." Guy said.

"Guy?" Sage asked.

"Haha?" They laughed.

"Look at us, we got life figured out?" Guy kissed Sage.

"Just making sure." Sage smiled. "It's our kids?"

It's nighttime for everyone...

"Art, why are you still in my mind?" Nina alone in her bed turned around trying to sleep.

"Nina, think about you since the very moment I met you." Art alone also turned around in his bed.

"Art, I missed you!" Nina made a phone call.

"Me too!" Art answered a phone call.

"Ah? Just wanted to say good night." Nina said.

"Yeah, right, uhm, me too." Art and Nina hung up a phone.

"Ah?" They looked a ceiling. "Ha." They fell asleep.

Beneath a moon Seagull's on sea...

"Lance?" Mona walked in a ship's office.

"You're on vacation again. Summer again." Lance smiled.

"I still have to talk about a wolf." Mona smiled.

"What is it, now?" Lance asked. "Wolf is gone."

"Yes, for some reason I keep having nightmares about him. As if, I should have put him behind bars?" Mona said. "Do you, think life, puts you through things? You know as if you had unfinished business? Kind of like condemning you for not putting someone behind bars. Dream him all the time. Dario has walked out the room, where I slept. And Wolf appears at my door. I wake up every time. Only, was no nightmare. Wolf did, uhm, take advantage of the situation. I never dare tell the cop. I thought being robbed from my office was crime enough. But, it's stolen much from me. More than pride?"

"I'm sorry, Mona." Lance hugged her.

"I so, needed this hug, Lance." Mona hugged him. "It's a wake me, every time. From a nightmare, into the world I once knew."

"And I got plenty more hug, just the same." Lance smiled.

"Haha. Love them all." Mona thanked.

"I know, you were taken advantage of, Mona." Vienna walked in the office. "But this picture, doesn't talk decent?"

"Vienna?" Mona turned around. "I'm sorry. My friend, your husband. I assure you, was all act."

"Is it, Mona, Lance, now?" Vienna must trust her husband and a friend?

"Is." They both answered.

"Is there ever a faithful friendship?" Vienna asked. "You know, I understand you both, all too well? But, is it me, but understanding me? With my own friends?"

"Haha." They laughed.

"Not a fair one, Vienna?" Lance smiled.

"But, when faithful." Vienna smiled.

"Ha?" Lance looked at his wife, she looked at him back.

"Hm? If I may?" Mona cleared her throat and smiled.

"Ah?" Lance and Vienna's attention was called.

"It's just papa, Mona." Lance said.

"Daddy." Vienna said.

"Haha." They laughed.

"How is that son of yours, Vienna?" Mona asked.

"Thanking, he's had a chance to a father, like Lance." Vienna said.

"Ha?" Lance smiled pride.

"Papa, he is." Mona smiled.

"Desmon, really can't have enough family, Mona." Vienna said.

"Haha." They laughed.

"I should thank you, Vienna." Mona smiled. "But this old crazy lady, family says."

"Haha." They laughed.

"Noo." Lance did scold.

"Vienna, wish I could open up to a woman about how my life, changed one day. But, man would understand me, lots better. Be supportive, as I need?" Mona turned to look a Lance with regret. "You know, Lance, I can talk to him about anything. And, he won't scare away?"

"Ha. Mona, I know I'm not much of a friend. It's not easy for me to understand what happened to you, when you aren't willing to talk to anyone else about it?" Vienna said. "You must know, I trust my husband? I can't allow you forget, beside friends needed you, I'm your wife, Lance?"

"I'm sorry, Vienna." Lance looked at his watch. "I'd meet my wife for lunch, Mona? You're welcome to join?"

"No. I've taken enough of your time. I'll meet with Art, and Carol. Not sure, I'm welcome in their circle, either?" She walked out the office.

"Lance, you might allow Mona find out, you've told me about she and Wolf?" Vienna asked still in the office.

"Mona will never trust me again." Lance held the door open for his wife.

"I know how much you care about Mona." Vienna followed outside. "At some point, she must know, she must talk to an expert about it? Someone about it. Victims need expert advice. So, they don't keep it all bottled up inside? It will help her about it. You know, flush it out, with something good.

Understand, no one else is at fault, but Wolf. No matter, what happened in that cabin, she was alone. Unable so to say, hang up a phone, close a door, yell out for help? Trusting Dario, if she knew, she could?"

"Let's, uhm, forget about my friend Mona?" Lance smiled. "Talk about love, over dinner?" He was at a table in a restaurant with view out to ocean.

"Oh, Lance, is it we talk love, still?" Vienna looked down at her plate, out to a darkened night with stars and Moon.

"Does the heart, grow old?" Lance asked with a smile.

"Yours keeps me, young." Vienna smiled.

"Those, love birds continue their love story." Mia was on a ship at kitchen doors.

"With Romance." Liam agreed walking to their table.

"Everywhere Mona is." Mia walked back in the kitchen. "I'll be near."

"Haha." Dario laughed. "Partners, is it. Guy, Mona?"

"I don't know anymore?" Mia smiled.

"Love that chef. Gets It right, every time." Dario walked in an office.

"Dario, can't get rid of you." Chef Jesse smiled.

"Nor, I, you." Dario at work, is on sail.

Entertainment on sea...

"Yeah, no matter how old you are, everyone is invited to sail." Jeramy smiled. "I was supposed to be on vacation. But,

Lance no idea, we comedians, go on vacation? Offered me a job for the weekend. I said, 'What better do I have to do? Pirates already booked pirate part of the sea?"

"Haha." An audience enjoyed a show.

"My wife, must rely on the ever message in a bottle?" Jeramy said.

"Haha." They laughed.

"Still waiting for that message?" Jeramy said. "Haha. I'm on sea, babe? Can't expect me to send a message, every second?"

"Haha." Everyone laughed.

"She works, so she can't come along with me, all the time." Jeramy said. "That woman talks so much, there wouldn't be any concentrating on anything, if she came along."

"Haha." They laughed.

"Catches me on every turn, trying to be funny. No, can't be funny around her. She wants to know everything? Sometimes, it has nothing to do with the girls? I love my wife, but you know some times that single friend, is the one getting you in trouble. With their, single's life? Boy? Haha. I tell him, but they still can't get to call his girl, the Mrs.? Why am I the one caught?"

"Haha." Everyone laughs.

"Yeah, I thought, finally vacation. Lay down all day, do nothing but party?" Jeramy said. "Na, na, none of my bosses is having that?"

"Haha." Everyone laughed.

"Gotta, make someone laugh, that isn't my family, friend," Jeramy said. "my girl?"

"Haha." They laughed.

"I see, you boys. Know what I'm talking about?" Jeramy said.

"Haha." They nodded with applaud.

"What are you laughing about? Nothing." Jeramy nodded on stage. "Nope."

"Haha." They laughed.

"Really, we laugh at our girl all the time. How they know what time we get home." Jeramy heard applause. "Every friend that calls, and about what?" Jeramy heard applause. "Mom asking, 'You tell your girl, I said hi, yeah, aha.' My girl doesn't deny she's listening. She'll take the phone, 'Just making sure your son, isn't talking to no other girl.'"

"Haha." Everyone laughs.

"Enjoy your cruise, have a drink with me sometime?" Jeramy smiled on stage. "Getting, to hang out with other than, Paul and Braxton. Life on sea."

"Haha." An audience applauds vacation with cheer.

"I might enjoy the sail, in my jokes?" Jeramy smiled. "Move onto sea?"

"Haha." A boat sails on sea.

At Carol and Art's room...

"Carol?" Mona was at the door.

"Mona." Carol opened the door. "Art and I were just asking about you?"

"Mona, with Lance, were you?" Art must scold.

"Just talking to Lance about, our friend Wolf?" Mona smiled in the living area.

"Who is Wolf?" Art and Carol asked.

"Ha? Sounds like some character taken out some book?" Carol laughed.

"Was." Mona smiled. "Vienna walked in the office asking for her husband. Carol, forgive Art and my friendship?"

"Oh, it's all right. You're not Darla?" Carol said.

"Not in the present time, no." Art said.

"Art, must we talk, Greg?" Carol asked.

"Ha?" Art and Carol laughed.

"You'd not allow, Darla and Art to talk?" Mona asked.

"Art allows I choose my friends too, Mona." Carol said. "We've been through enough to allow ourselves make a mistake, only to regret. You know, brings us apart."

"Hm." Art smiled.

"Art, you better not be smiling because you've disagreed, about all Carol's said? Love." Mona said.

"Ha?" They all laughed in hallways.

"Is it the weekend again?" Dario is in the restaurant. "I recommend the Chef's Breakfast." He had a table to attend.

"I'll have that." Mona smiled.

"And we've already ordered." Art said about Carol and he.

"I'll be back with your breakfast." Dario walked away.

"Seagull's. Just the place to escape to sea." Art said. "We should escape to Island Cruise next time?"

"You will be paying?" Mona asked. "I will definitely, make it."

"Haha." They laughed.

"Truth is, with all kinds of work, we don't have time for any more vacationing." Art said.

"Oh, I'll make sure we fit it in." Carol said.

"Haha." They laughed.

"Mona, you know my friends keep asking about you?" Carol asked. "I'd like to answer them someday, about that date?"

"Oh, I like my single life." Mona said. "I suppose the day I find a guy who agrees to all I say, I'll date him."

"Haha." They laughed.

"Date him. You've heard it, Carol. A guy is ready to marry the girl, cause he's serious and, Mona, you've just thought date?" Art asked. "You will be serious, about dating? I mean, why would anyone date, if serious doesn't bring you to the altar?"

"Art, of course, I'll get married someday. What assures, you'll marry the first person you meet?" Mona asked. "Party animal, not all people are the same?"

"Second?" Art said.

"Ha?" Carol laughed with them.

"Oh, because we dated, Art?" Mona said. "Don't worry Carol, our friendship meant more?"

"Ha?" Carol laughed. "You know, Mona it's all right. We'll never understand when we talk, not around Art?"

"Until, Carol, I have a date?" Mona asked.

"Ha? Might work?" Carol said.

"Girls?" Art asked. "One of you must make me look good?"

"Really, Art, thank you for being my friend. And, Carol, I know it's not easy sitting in the same table with your husband's ex-girlfriend, he insists, on it?" Mona said.

"You're going through a rough time?" Art explained.

"Oh, Mona, even if it was all fun and games?" Carol held her hand.

"Nice of you, Carol." Mona smiled. "You must know gossip, does sell?"

"Haha?" Carol laughed. "If anything, real would?"

"Mona, always accusing." Art said. "Me?"

"Haha." They laughed.

"Of course you, author." Mona said.

"Haha." They laughed.

"Knew you had reason for it." Art laughed with wife and friend.

"Looks like Art's table, is a party?" Vienna laughed with her husband at their table on the other side of a ship's restaurant.

"Painting, inspired art by, Vienna." Lance smiled about decor.

"You just show me your love, everywhere." Vienna thanked. *"This painting is about a girl waving bye to life on land from a ship."* She looked at a painting on wall at their table.

"Might be to, her lover?" Lance asked.

"In the eyes of the beholder." Vienna said. *"Inspired by Vienna, is what you've said."*

"Love it, Vienna." Lance smiled.

Days later. On board...

"Your wife, Lance?" Mona had dinner with Lance.

"She would have tea with a friend." Lance smiled. *"How are you, friend?"*

"How is Sapphire?" Mona asked.

"Mona?" Lance asked. *"We agreed, we'd trust each other, private."*

"Wolf, was never love, Lance." Mona said.

"I know." Lance said. *"And don't you be funny about it. Someone might just pass by, hear about what's going on between Sapphire and I?"*

"I doubt, it's still present." Mona smiled. *"Though, I'd understand if, you were still in love?"*

"Why?" Lance asked. "I've heard you're a serious girl?"

"You remember when I was a young girl, Lance?" Mona asked. "I used to walk in your office. I used to want to run out crying. I'd find Sapphire in your office. I didn't know, but I speculated something was going on between you two. With all the girls walking in your office with all kinds of excuses, thought you might be one of those men, who dated lots. Even though married. Was my naïve, jealous heart. For someone, I respected much. Loved you, you knew?"

"Of course. We'd spend hours talking." Lance said. "One can't help to feel close, that close to you. Maybe, Sapphire? Why explain to a young naïve girl?"

"Haha? Is that why you never did, explain? This naïve girl, only understood love is between two, faithful. You'd broken my heart, with your unfaithful. Why must a decent good man like you, betray real love? Like father to me." Mona cried. "Only you, weren't my daddy. Thought it was my love, you didn't want to lose, without any explanation?"

"Haha?" They laughed once a forgotten mistake.

"So, I ask you forgive me, for walking in your office like that. You'd say, it's all right. I'd excuse myself, after letting you know, as soon as you were done with your busy meetings, I'd be put front of your agenda, again." Mona said.

"My office, would never allow time for it." Lance said. "But, with someone like you, my life became my office."

"Yes, I'd get that message across, at some point." Mona smiled. "I needed a friend to talk to, you were it."

"Anyone might ask, and they did. Why talk to someone like me, call me friend?" Lance said. "Twice your age."

"Not, quite. Teens, grown-ups wouldn't understand, any? What I talked about, serious." Mona said. "Until, it became serious. Now I needed you more than ever."

"Now, we held hands, kissed." Lance said. "Mistake of love."

"My mistake." Mona said. "Should have explained that hug."

"Mistake. Should have understood it, as such." Lance a married man, did regret.

"All a mistake, Lance. I'd never, you'd never allow anything more than talk and laughs, happen. Because of Wolf, my life became sinful?" Mona said. "I, uhm, understood in time, was a mistake. Would have lost, your friendship, Vienna's. I'd invested so much more than money. Friendship, for us to call ourselves, strangers? Have you, Lance explained, to Vienna? I've understood?"

"Hm? Couldn't allow that moment in your life, be the only. I was a way to escape, keep your reality, from an unreal, torment." Lance looked at his coffee. "Moment, left in the past, as should be. Enjoying our lives as we did once before any of it, are you enjoying tea?"

"Yes, you know I love my tea." Mona smiled. "Lance, I can't forgive myself, for crossing that friendship line. I live every day to, regret it?"

"Mona, it wasn't you crossed it, it was you held on to something. That something, was me." Lance held her hand. "It's all right. We've understood? Sometimes people need more than just a sail, through Lance Sea?"

"I hate that I turn human, again." Mona smiled. "Thank you. Just glad you've known me human, before wolf. You had scratched me out your, friend's list."

"Haha." They laughed.

"Mona, don't express yourself like that, about you." Lance smiled. "There is only one wolf, and that's Wolf. You're, Mona. Even Monica."

"Ooh, don't you call me out?" Mona smiled.

"Haha." They laughed.

"I live to regret it too. Should have understood, something wasn't right." Lance said.

"Like you said, there's only one guilty, that's wolf. We probably would have made that mistake, just the same." Mona said.

"Mona, had we?" Lance held her hand.

"Oh, no." Mona looked up. "We'd have never held hands, like I needed. Human love."

"Remember Monica, my Monica." Lance said.

"It's a good thing, we're both wide awake." Mona looked down at her tea.

"Hm?" They both looked at each other.

"Do me a favor, remind yourself our life remains uninterrupted. Only mistake, was ours?" Lance asked.

"Wolf never existed. Sure, nightmares talk pendant." Mona smiled. "Only mistake, was ours, Lance."

"Yeah, I think Wolf has gotten enough attention." Lance said. "A walk down boat pathway?"

"I'd love that." Mona said. "Miss those whales."

"Oh, whale?" Lance said.

"Haha." They laughed.

"Theater is next." Lance said.

"Ooh, love you." Mona walked down boat path with Lance. "Love those night ocean moon walks too."

"I hate to take my husband back, Mona." Vienna walked to them.

"Mona, time to get back to the room." Somra was also front of them.

"Good night, Mona." Lance took his wife's hand.

"Good night." Mona watched them walk away." Mona smiled. "Somra, time to get back to my room."

"Walked the whole ship, had foods of every kind." Somra walked with Mona in entrance doors.

"Haha." Mona laughed with Somra.

"Watched Whales chase each other back in water...moon, till it was nighttime." Somra was front of Mona's room.

"Ha, Somra sometimes I think your life is more exciting than my own." Mona was in her room.

"For a brief moment, it is." Somra said outside the room. "Will Lance join you for breakfast? Must I make a wakeup call?"

"I believe Summer and Sam joined a cruise." Mona smiled.

"Mona, do remember you're single." Somra watched a door close.

"Haha. What am I still doing single?" Mona laughed.

In Seagull's hallways...

"Something happened between Mona and friend Wolf." Carol said. "I, not at fault--"

"And Mona needs us right now." Art said. "You will forgive?"

"I'm not used to sharing you with someone else, Art, but of course. I will forgive, you." Carol smiled.

"Lance agreed he'd spend time with her at the theater, so we have the night to our own." Art smiled.

"Where are Magda, Guy," Carol asked. "hate to put them all in a same sentence, but where's Darla? Don't know what's going on? But not the best situation to be alone, in all this?"

"They, uhm, have no idea about it?" Art said.

"Why, Art?" Carol was front of him. "Thought you and Guy talked lots, slipped out into conversation? Not talking anymore?"

"It's tough enough for us to understand this?" Art said.

"Oh, so it's something, Guy wouldn't understand. Randy, what would he say about this?" Carol said. "Have a feeling, Wolf would like Mona as far away from, friends as possible?" She turned to look at her husband with handbag in her hand. "Astrid?" She got her phone. "I, uhm, have no idea, what's

happened to Mona. Think, you're another friend, Wolf would like to stay from Mona?"

"You've found out, Mona and I are closer, than you knew?" Astrid said. "Why I'm calling, find out. Need we, converse with, Wolf?"

"Carol, must I tell all?" Art was front of her. "Talking to Wolf, won't be necessary, anymore. He's uhm, in paradise."

"Ah?" Carol looked at Art front of her. "Astrid, need not worry about it."

"Then, I'll continue on land." Astrid said. "You must come visit, again."

"I will." Carol said.

"How are you still friends?" Art asked. "How are any of us, still friends?"

"Guys, door is open?" Greg is at the door. "Just wanted to ask about Mona?"

"She's doing better." Art smiled. "Giana and you becoming distant, friends."

"Still, friends." Greg smiled. "Bethany and I had breakfast."

"Yes, of course, she told me." Carol looked at Art.

"Well, we're going to see if we catch any whales?" Greg said. "Friends." He walked away.

"Thought now that I didn't see him at the office, he'd be less annoying?" Art said. "How does he do this? Right, Bethany's—"

"Father, Art?" Carol held his tie.

"I." Art said.

"Ah?" They looked at each other.

"Feels like, not all, is lost between us?" Art said.

"Ah?" Carol let his tie go. "No, it's, uhm, not?" She turned away.

"Carol?" Art turned her toward him. "Don't run from this?"

"Ah?" Carol looked at him.

"Love you." Art kissed her. "You've distinguished, Carol." He smiled.

"You're looking more like yourself." Carol kissed him.

"Ah?" Art a tall white guy, brown eyes, in suit and tie asked. "Kissed the right guy, this time."

"This here, is love, Art." Carol smiled. "Not, friendship."

"Guys?" Mona is at the door.

"Door, remains open." Carol pointed handbag walked to the door.

"Haha." Art and Carol laughed.

"Sorry, Mona, Greg walked by to let us know, Bethany would be spending the day with dad." Carol said.

"Sure, seems to take the role of papa." Mona smiled. "So, how will we start our day today?"

"Mona, don't think we're doing this because of all that's happened to you?" Carol said. "We want a free ticket to Island Cruise."

"Haha?" Mona laughed. "It's friendship that will cost you."

"Haha." They laughed.

"Breakfast, we've had none?" Carol said. "Then, we can walk stores take something home, remember this trip? Maybe send some painted art, home. Just enjoy the crafts?"

"Ooh, Carol, you've planned some day." Mona smiled.

"Learned it from Art. He's a good date." Carol smiled.

"Haha. Ooh, hope there's more guys like you out here?" Mona said.

"I've taken this one." Carol held his arm.

"Table for, three?" Mia is a hostess.

...

"Desmon is, uhm, ready with his ship, for a sail across Sea Lance." Art said at the table.

"Well, no one can," Carol looked threw a menu. "deny now."

"Ah?" Mona looked at them. "No." She smiled.

"Congratulate, Desmon for me?" Art asked.

"Us, Art?" Carol held his hand on the table.

"Us?" Art smiled at Mona.

"Oh, you will let us know whose child, he is?" Carol asked. "Before promotion does it? Haha. You know, how nothing escapes them?"

"Haha. Mine, of course." Mona laughed.

"Oh, Mona, I was thinking we were friends." Carol said. "Summer, Sam, they do know this?"

"Ah?" Mona looked at them.

"Ha." Art looked at Mona.

"No, of course they know as much as you do." Mona hurried to say.

"Well, Art, think it's time we got ourselves some new friends?" Carol asked. "Guy, I've heard talks to, well, at least Summer?"

"So, same wouldn't be in trouble, if we talked to her?" Art said.

"Guys?" Mona looked at the menu as if she had no troubles.

"Ah?" Carol and Art looked at each other.

"What, if, Guy got there on time, Carol. What then?" Art whispered.

"What is it you're discussing?" Mona put down the menu.

"What, we'll be sharing, of course?" Carol hurried to answer about breakfast.

...

"Want to thank you for spending the day with me." Mona said. "I will bring something back with me, for Desmon. Can't wait for my grandkids. Forgotten how to hold a baby. Years ago, I carried little Desmon in my arms."

"Oh, it'll come right back to you, once that baby brings back baby memories." Carol said. *"I can't believe, Desmon isn't married, but already a ship?"*

"With many ideas, it's still not all that ready built." Mona said. *"Someday, maybe grandson baby will join a first cruise?"*

"Ha. Can't wait." Art smiled.

"Yeah, and you're not Grandpa." Mona said.

"Ha." Art looked at Mona.

"Desmon's baby, we know that much." Carol smiled. *"I can't wait to take that cruise. Desmon's world must be, different from your world, Mona?"*

"Desmon is different from mom. Then again, they say behind a great man, stands a great woman." Mona smiled.

"And, who is the lucky girl?" Art asked.

"Exactly my question?" Carol must know. *"He has brought her home. That usually means, serious?"*

"Oh, she's a lovely young lady." Mona said. *"She's got blue eyes, blonde hair. A personality, that speaks all, lady. But she hates me."*

"Ah?" Art and Carol looked at her.

"We, uhm, have different point of views?" Mona smiled in trouble.

"Oh? Oh?" Carol said.

"Haha." They laughed.

"Find that hard to believe?" Art said.

"Oh, because at work, everyone hates boss." Mona explained.

"Oh, Art, you're a difficult man to work with?" Carol said.

"Haha." They laughed.

"He, is, Mona." Carol said.

"Oh, I know." Mona wasn't arguing. *"He must hurry someone from her sip. And, make sure that gun, hits the target?"*

"Ha?" Carol laughed. *"Art, really?"*

"She thinks story, she can make up her own?" Art said.

"Ha?" Mona laughed.

"Hm." Art had proven a point.

"Oh?" Mona tried to laugh. *"Version."*

"Haha." They laughed.

"Oh, but don't mind me. You've told how Art, really is a romantic, when it comes to dates?" Mona said.

"Not, even begun." Carol said.

"Ah?" Mona looked at Carol.

"Ah?" Carol looked at Mona.

"Someone, must talk nice about me?" Art with hands on his side asked.

"Oh, look Bethany, there's another one of me?" Greg walked to the crowd of friends.

"Haha." Bethany and Greg laughed.

"Where?" Art turned around.

"Oh, you know we're looking into a mirror, when we're front of each other." Greg said.

"Haha?" Both guys laughed. "I don't see it."

"Haha." Everyone laughed.

"Giana went looking for Randy." Greg said. "Left Bethany and I alone. Was all my fault, we stole her for a bit. Some kind of family time?" He looked at his daughter Bethany.

"Oh, dad?" Bethany smiled.

"We have theater, Carol?" Art reminded. "Mona, you'll meet with Lance?" He excused himself walking away with his wife and daughter.

"Greg, how have you been?" Mona asked.

"Well, with Giana dating at the office. Thinking of getting a job, where there is no office. You know, avoid, a girl leave me for the other office guy?"

"Haha?" They laughed.

"Would like to pay for a ship's room, someday?" Greg asked.

"Ooh, Greg, you have to give it up someday?" Mona said.

"Haha?" They laughed.

"Art, is right, Lance will be looking for me in a bit." Mona said.

"Mona, you're all right." Greg hugged her. "You will be?" He pushed her away to look at her.

"Am, thanks. You know, with real friend like, you."
Mona walked away.

"You're my, uhm," Greg quieted down to a whisper.
"inspiration." He with hands in pockets watched her walk away.

Inside a hallway's room...

"You haven't spent any time with me, Mona." Somra
smiled in Mona's room. "You sure you'll be all right, with Mr.
Scavo?"

"Somra, can't thank you enough for being here for me.
You may walk around the ship, tell me later, how it's been
upgraded? All kinds of tech and décor." Mona smiled. "Tonight,
Mr. Scavo has invited me for a night of theater. Know how
much, I love theater."

"I, do." Somra walked out the room.

"Mona, just saw a man walk out your room, why
entertain with anyone else?" Lance walked in her room.

"That was Somra." Mona smiled. "I'm all ready to enjoy
this night out my room?"

"Vienna, will enjoy night swim with friends." Lance
smiled.

"I've heard some couples enjoy their time away from
each other. Never thought it true. Didn't realize," Mona and
Lance walked down hallways. "Desmon and I did the same
thing. Only, I knew where his escapes were headed, with
another."

"Why not forget, our cheat?" Lance smiled.

"Ah?" Mona looked at him. "Not sure, it will ever be safe to laugh about it."

"We're, here. Theater." Lance opened the door for Mona.

"Thank you." Mona walked in, he followed behind.

Music began to play below theater stage...

"Art, thank you for including theater in our vacation." Carol was front of theater doors.

"Oh, but this isn't just one more night of theater." Art opened the door.

Music quieted down with a beginning of a story. In the dark a shot is fired. Another man falls to the floor.

"Great, like a detective, our story begins backward." Art said.

"Haha." Carol laughed.

On stage...

"I've been left, widow!" A woman cried on her knees, her hands grabbed on to a body's clothes. "Don't leave me alone, in this world!" She cried on him but heard no heartbeat.

"Woman, he's gone now." Jimmy a name tag reads on a sheriff's shirt. He helped her up. "We'll catch, a criminal."

"Thank you, Jimmy." A widow looked in his eyes.

Island Cruise. A restaurant's view is boat path and endless ocean...

"Like Seagull's, plans cross path with Island Cruise." Art smiled at a table on a third floor.

"Haha." Nina saw Island Cruise wasn't the only ship on ocean.

"We escape the parents." Art said.

"Art, thanks for joining me for dinner." Nina said. "It's late."

"You know me, I don't have a girl." Art said.

"Why?" Nina asked.

"I date, girls don't want a serious relationship." Art said.

"Is it, Art, the girls?" Nina asked.

"Why would you doubt me?" Art asked.

"I've dated enough to know, guys aren't committed." Nina said.

"Know this has nothing to do with my brother Guy. He's a married man." Art asked.

"Guy once he found out, about you and I, he didn't want anything to do with me. He kept breaking up with me. He kept disappearing on me. I had to break up with him, mean it." Nina said.

"Thought it was he who—" Art said.

"I don't believe Guy didn't know what he was doing, once he disappeared from my life. Besides, he'd met Sage. Was in love. How would his mind ever stop thinking about her? Even when he was with me?" Nina said.

"Just because someone thinks about someone, doesn't mean, they forget the one they're with." Art said.

"I'd like to have known that, when I was with Guy. I was jealous, of every girl that was next to him, had been part of his life. Wanted to be the only. I, uhm?" Nina turned away. "Don't mean, I'm still in love with him. I just meant—"

"You're not, anymore." Art said. "It's not right for you and I to meet like this. You know, we almost fell in love, before you met brother Guy. And this looks like we're betraying him. After all, he did ask you, to be his girl. I barely—"

"Why, Art, didn't you ask me to be your girlfriend?" Nina asked. "That day we met, I'm sure for a split second, we lived so much more than just that stare?"

"The circumstances?" Art said.

"Right, no one will ever forget, I've stolen." Nina said. "But, we got home at some point?"

"Hm, was too soon?" Art asked. "Then you'd met my brother."

"Was, busy." Nina said.

"Still, stares back and forth—" Art said.

"Right, he's moved on." Nina said. "Ah. Were still two strangers to me. Then he'd asked me to be his girlfriend. Can't even remember if I said, yes? If he asked, 'Why do you need to think about it?'"

"It's been years. You'd think, you'd never forget?" Art said. "Betrayal, was an answer."

"We both know, that's not true." Nina said. "How to expect a girl to imagine a love story, never was? And with a complete stranger?"

"Were we, you and I?" Art asked. "Forgotten me."

"Why not, you both had forgotten about me. All I could think about, was throw those diaries in the trash, the memory of me, in your heart." Nina said.

"Nina, you just threw them in the trash, as if you weren't part of them?" Art asked. *"What did you write in them, anyway?"*

"That you never called again." Nina said. *"I wanted to forget it all. And, it worked. Don't have facts."*

"Yeah, well since you were part of it, like a heart, we have the other half. One can't possibly, have lived a same dream?" Art looked at her.

"Right. A broken-hearted chain." Nina looked out to ocean.

"Guy calling it, evidence, Nina?" Art asked.

"Evidence, is what he's gifted Sage, with that wedding ring." Nina said.

"What's wrong?" Art asked. *"Like you're still heartbroken?"*

"Let's, uhm, Art, forget this?" Nina with plead held his hand.

"Hm?" Art looked at her hand on his then at her.

"I'm sorry." Nina hurried to move her hand from his. *"How could you have forgotten me? I mean, I understand, Guy up and fell back in love with Sage. Who can blame him for it, if I was not the girl he looked for. But, you and I we were friends, Art? Did it ever occur to you, I needed a friend, ever?"*

"Did you?" Art asked.

"No." Nina said. "But I wanted my best friend there. Tell him, how my day went. How I didn't get a job, kept losing them?"

"Why?" Art asked.

"Last, one my friend and I ended up throwing pizzas at each other, instead of selling them." Nina said.

"Ha? What?" Art laughed. "Why?"

"For a guy." Nina said.

"Sage?" Art asked.

"We'd found out, we dated the same guy." Nina said. "I mean, we had no idea, we had."

"Oh, boy?" Art said.

"Oh, brother?" Nina looked at him. "Like every time I fall in love, something's wrong. Can't ever get it right?"

"Right?" Art looked at her.

"Never could understand, Guy's reaction to our friendship. You know, still feel like we're doing something wrong? When I know, he's in love with Sage?" Nina said.

"He is." Art said.

"You don't talk to her, much?" Nina said.

"She's a serious girl." Art said. "I still have thoughts somewhere else."

"Where?" Nina asked.

"Hm?" Art looked at her.

"Guy, why would he care I moved on, with anyone, even with you? If he's all in love with Sage?" Nina asked. "It's not like

I'm trying to get him jealous. Cause any uncomfortable feeling, when we're in the same room, while you and his girl are there? Just know it's over. Why does he act like it isn't? He knows you're a good guy. I feel like asking him sometimes—"

"What?" Art asked.

"If he's really not in love with Sage? You know, like he tells. Doesn't act like it, when I'm around, and with you?" Nina said. "Feel his unlove, all over again? Once he's remembered, Sage by his side?"

"Why, tell me this?" Art looked out to sea. "That's my brother you're talking about. What do you want me to say, Nina?" He was now next to boat rails with Nina. "Like you'd like me to tell you, maybe it's his heartbreak, doing the talking. He's a married man." He walked away.

"Art?" Nina got his arm.

"What?" Art turned around. "Will we be spending years, talking how I known all our lives, you're in love with my brother. I should understand, how you're feeling? Remind you he's a married man? I'm not doing it, Nina?"

"Why, because you have feelings for me? Because you hate me, for falling in love with your brother, thinking you had no idea, I was alive?" Nina asked.

"No. Don't hate you." Art said. "It's just all, wrong. I'll only end up?"

"What?" Nina asked.

"We, talk too much. We'll only end up realizing, in every word we say, we tell how we really feel about each other?"

"Hm?" Nina looked at him. "That you're not like him? What I mean, is when you get married, you won't be in the same room with your girl, looking at another? Trying to remember, you never even liked her. Once you've looked at your girl by your side?"

"Same girl, you?" Art looked at her holding her arm.

"Yeah, me." Nina held on to boat rails moving her arm from his hand.

"No, I will never look at another girl, Nina." Art said.

"It's a good thing you're not married, yet. I wouldn't believe you." Nina saw he still looked at her.

"Hm?" Art didn't deny it.

"Ha?" They laughed.

"Having a good night." Guy stood front middle of them.

"Hm?" They both turned to look at him.

"I was, just on my way to look for Sage." Guy gestured to a boat path that led to front of a ship.

"Guy?" Sage walked to him. "Is it you're still jealous over your ex?"

"Sage, no. No." Guy turned to look at her.

"Then, why not allow, Nina finally date your brother Art." Sage asked.

"Ah?" They turned to look at her.

"You know, Nina, how you interrupted, something?" Sage said. "Right, we'd like a chance at a decent family?"

"Was exactly my question?" Nina looked at Guy.

"Nina?" Guy looked at her.

"Guy?" Sage ran to the front of the boat.

"Go, ahead, Guy, find her?" Nina asked him.

"I'll, uhm, find her?" Art watched them look at each other.

"Ah?" Guy and Nina looked at each other.

"Guy, is that okay?" Art asked.

"No, Art, thanks. You continue your talk with, Nina." Guy looked at Art. *"I'll go find my wife."* He looked at Nina.

"Do you see it?" Nina asked. *"He's allowed her to run, hide in a crowd. What is it, with him? Still in love with me? Why marry, Sage?"*

"Nina, you'd forget about him?" Art asked.

"Oh, why is it so easy for you to recriminate something, it's so hard to do?" Nina asked. *"Art, I hate to hurt your feelings. Have lost your friendship with truth. Spent time with your brother, and it wasn't just chit chats, about everything? Wasn't sharing a drink, movies? We spent time alone, as a couple. Doesn't hurt the same to have thrown one diary, like another?"*

"Well, thanks for your honesty?" Art looked at her lips talking. He looked at ship floor.

"Art, I don't know what's going on. But my heart still pains over all this. Thinking it's all my fault? You and Guy aren't any close?" Nina said.

"Na, we never were?" Art lied.

"Because you've just found out, just how much I loved your brother, you hate me?" Nina said.

"I, don't?" Art said. "All right, so it hurts. Because all that time, this time, I thought you were falling in love with me. And when I was looking at anyone else, not your friends, either, you were looking at my brother?"

"Weren't?" Nina asked. "What about that waitress girl, Mia, you talk like you were more than just client?"

"Hm, Nina, come on?" Art smiled. "You're acting like jealous girlfriend now?"

"Ah?" Nina said.

"She's like, so much older for this young guy." Art said.

"Ha?" They laughed.

"She's, like mama, to me." Art said.

"Ha?" They looked at each other.

"So, we, uhm, continue on that walk?" Art asked. "Unless you want to party?"

"We'll end up falling in love to some slow song?" Nina said.

"Right." Art and Nina walked down boat path talking and laughing.

"Then, someday I'd met my best friend. Couldn't believe the moon I looked out to every night, was the same moon, he slept under. Knew no matter where in this world, I was? I really never was alone."

"Haha." They laughed front of a ship.

"Sounds like bedtime to me." Somra stood middle front of them with hands held front of him.

"Ah?" Art and Nina turned to look at him.

"Mona said, no matter how old you are, you're still kids." Somra shrugged.

"Haha?" They laughed.

"Ah, no we're not." Nina said.

"Think, we should get some sleep, for tomorrow?" Art walked with Nina back to their rooms.

"Hm." Somra smiled front a ship watching friends walk away.

In a club...

"Not a drink more." Oso said to Guy.

"Who are you, my dad?" Guy asked.

"If you need me to parent?" Oso said.

"Haha." They laughed.

"We agreed gang would hang out tomorrow. We gotta look good." Oso reminded. "Brother Art will turn us in with the parents?"

"Right, brother Art. Perfect child." Guy said.

"No matter how perfect Art is, still not you, Guy." Oso said.

"Just making sure, you knew we would hang out tomorrow?" Art was front of them.

"Ooh, you heard me?" Oso said. "It's all right, I'm still Oso."

"Haha." They laughed.

"Nina, for the guys, might we someday agree on something?" Sage asked.

"On, something, like what?" Nina asked Sage.

"Friends." Sage asked.

"Yeah, friends." Uzma put up a drink. "Sorry, we're done with this drinking!" He put the drink on the bar.

"Think, Uzma is a bit drunk?" Oso saw.

"A little." Uzma said.

"That's it, you're not drinking tomorrow." Oso walked out the club with friends.

"No, drinking for anyone. Pool party!" Uzma yelled down hallway.

"Your friend's gonna be all right?" A security asked.

"Oh, he better." Oso said.

"Haha." They laughed.

"Parenting, here." Oso said.

Mona, Desmon is it business that brings them together?

"I'd like to move on with my life." Mona smiled in her home.

"We still have pendant things." Desmon said.

"Anything, we need to take care of, you have your men for." Mona said. "There's no reason for us to see each other again."

"There is family." Desmon said.

"Family knows, where my home is." Mona said. *"So, Desmon, let's make things go smooth as they can? Allow ourselves not to meet like this."*

"All right, Mona. Though we could be friends, after we—" Desmon said.

"After, married couple?" Mona said. "Desmon, don't make me call Loretta and allow she find out, you're not that into her. Unless, she just decided to blind herself so she may continue to believe, she's the decent in this picture?"

"I believe we've divorced." Desmon said.

"Have." Mona said. "I apologize, but I'm not the only girl in your life, Desmon. Had I known pretty boys, really do get any girl they'd like, I'd married a man who wasn't. I'd stayed married."

"You're a beautiful woman, Mona." Desmon said.

"Doesn't work, there's always a prettier girl, beside me." Mona smiled.

"I had to apologize." Desmon said.

"I suppose, we both do." Mona said. "Loretta is it?"

"I'll answer, out there." Desmon walked out Mona's home.

"Thanks." Mona closed a door. "Hello?" She answered a call.

"Mona, I need help. About Blue Bay Hotel?" Art in his office, at his desk front of a computer, explained.

"Oh, thought it a personal call." Mona said.

"Haha." Friends talk. A phone call is a connection.

"Let's not get in trouble with the other one." Art asked.

"You're married, I'm single." Mona said.

"You know." Art did remind.

"So, Art, what is it? Will I need to come in the office? And, which one?" Mona asked.

"Not Create World." Art said.

Months later. Mona returns to ice skating...

"I can't wait to go out there." Mona told Dario.

"It's become time, Mona." Darla said.

"Thank you." Mona went to an ice skate entrance.

"You're killing it." Dario smiled.

"Thank you." Mona skated onto ice.

"Ha!" An audience applauds with cheer.

Music plays. Mona skates a solo...

"Moment I met you, my world became about you. I could think about nothing else, without making you part of my life. Once I met you, everything in my life became about you. I was obsessed with you. Once I met you, I had no family, friend, than you. We were angels in heaven, we were accomplice in all, right, wrong!" A man's voice sang to music.

"Ah!" Mona falls.

"Ah?" A crowd cheers Mona's fall.

"Hm?" Mona stands up and puts her hands up side of her. She skates off ice.

"It's okay, Mona." Art is at the benches. "People fall all the time."

"Not, I." Mona continued to her dressing room. "Ah?" She looked at herself in the mirror in cry.

"Mona?" Guy walked in her dressing room.

"Guy?" Mona turned around.

"Mona, sorry about that fall." Magda with smile walked behind Guy.

"Guy, must you continue to interrupt my life?" Mona asked.

"Theater. It was ice. Magda," Guy turned around to look at his wife. "and I, decided to watch it. There is, Mona skating." He explained advertisement. "We thought we might support, your act?"

"Yes, Mona, not trying to, uhm, what are you thinking this is?" Magda asked.

"I've fallen front of everyone. And, you were there, Magda, to witness my fall?" Mona cried.

"Mona, I know we started all wrong, by meeting as complete strangers. But let's not? Be complete strangers?" Magda asked.

"I'd say enemies." Mona smiled. "All right, you insist, this is friendship. Thank you for insisting on watching my fall?"

"We'll get out your life, now, Mona. It's what I've understood from all this. No answered calls?" Guy said.

"Your wife is right next to you, Guy?" Mona asked.

"Thing about my wife, she trusts me. Might be all wrong?" Guy explained.

"I'm, right next to him, Mona, right." Magda smiled. "Very well, just don't cry because we've become strangers to your life."

"No?" Mona said. "I fell out there. Felt like the entire world would do nothing but condemn my mistake? My competition, cheer about it."

"Ha?" They laughed with Mona.

"Thanks. Means all that to me, you noticed?" Mona said.

"Ha?" They laughed.

"I have to head out there, after falling. I have a duet dance." Mona said.

"We've," Magda looked at her husband. "heard."

"Have." Guy said. "My best friend continues, traitor."

"Ha?" They all laughed.

"Guy, are you ever serious about, how you feel about Art? Being a traitor?" Mona asked.

"He's not dating my wife, Magda." Guy smiled. "And I did think it personal. Traitor."

"Mona your time is up." Dario walked in the dressing room. "Guys."

"We've spoken in the hallways." Magda smiled at Dario.

"We're on our way out." Guy held Magda's hand and walked out with her.

"This time, your act is over," Dario said. "if you fall."

"Thanks for the reminder." Mona said.

"Mona, seriously, must I?" Dario asked.

"Haha?" They laughed.

"Worry not about, my heart?" Mona smiled.

"Not when Guy's around." Dario said.

Mona is back on ice...

"I like a chase. I like a chase. I like a chase." A voice of a girl sing is heard as Mona skates three steps on ice. Art follows behind. "When I'm crying out." Mona turns around front of Art.

"Ah?" Art tries to stop front of Mona moving hands and feet trying not to fall nor bump into her.

"Ah?" Mona skates away again followed by Art with a same ice dance.

"Her hair is a mess." A man's voice continues sing. "Her clothes don't match. She's failed a test. Her skate's a fall. And she's crying out. She likes a chase. She likes a chase. She likes a chase. When she's crying out." A man continues to sound throughout an ice theater.

"Ah?" Mona turns around.

"Ah?" Art holds her in dance position.

"Her hair's a mess. She doesn't match. She's failed a test. Her skate's a fall. And she's crying out." Song plays as Art and Mona, a couple dance. "She likes a chase. She likes a chase. She likes a chase. When she's crying out."

"Ha!" An audience cheers.

Five guys dance skate to them, circling them in. Sideway they make a stop. Another song…

"I want a guy who loves me. And isn't in love with himself." Song plays as Mona skates to a guy who is looking at himself in the mirror. Guy closes the mirror and skates away. "I want a guy who isn't on the phone, and with another girl." Song continues as Mona skates to a guy on the phone. The guy skates away joining the first guy. "I want a guy who tells me, he loves me so." Song continues as Mona skates to a guy who pretends yell and gestures to her as she skates to him. He skates with the other two guys. "I don't want a guy who skates around, ignoring I'm part of his life." Song continues as Mona skates to a Guy who skates alone as the star of the show. He skates joining the other three. "I want a guy who isn't crime." Song continues as Mona skates to a guy who counts money. The guy skates with the others. "I want a guy who is all mine." Song continues as Mona skates to Art who skates to her. "I want to fall in love, with a guy who keeps me from everyone, closer to him."

"Ah!" Art skates chasing the guys skating around Mona away.

"I'm in love with a man, who loves me back." Song continues as Mona and Art skate together.

"We want love like, that." Song continues as five guys skate toward Mona and Art circling them in dance again.

"We conclude our show." Jeramy is on ice. "Enjoy our next show on ice." Jeramy smiled. "After dinner?"

"Mona, will you ever give your heart away?" Art was front of her on ice. "Again?"

"It'll be a first time, Art." Mona smiled. "Can't give your heart away, to someone doesn't want it?"

"You feel better about that fall?" Art asked still on ice.

"I wanted to be perfect." Mona smiled. "My first fall."

"Mona, I'm sorry about your fall." Carol skated to Art.

"Thanks." Mona said. "Can't believe no one missed that one?" She skates away.

"Not professional, still want to join in the ice?" Carol explained her skates.

"You've taken classes." Art smiled.

"Have." Carol held his hand and kissed him.

"That is not part of the show?" Jeramy still held a microphone.

"Haha." Everyone laughed.

"We should get out of here?" Art with Carol skated away.

"Lifetime on ice." Guy was still at benches.

"We can't ever tell the complete story, Guy." Art said. "For what it's worth, I am sorry."

"Never, friend, apologize for love." Guy said. "Mona, once did say."

"But, when a friend, brother." Art said.

"Ah?" Guy looked at him for a moment. "The girls, have their own war, Art?"

"They do." Art like Guy turned to look at them.

"Haha." Mona and Carol laughed at benches.

"Looks like we should make peace?" Mona whispered to Carol.

"Should?" Carol saw Art and Guy watched them laugh. *"Is there anything you don't do, Mona?"*

"When, a spoil." Mona did thank Alvaro.

"Guy, I believe the show has ended?" Magda walked to join him. *"Do you miss skating?"*

"Do." Guy said.

"Thanks for coming to the show." Art left.

"Nice one." Magda said.

"Thanks." Art turned back.

"Some teenage years." Magda smiled. *"Was it dance on ice with, Shandra?"*

"Know me." Guy smiled. *"One day, I'd met Magda."*

"Barely in your life, Guy. Know you've made your decision to marry me, but is it I, in your heart?" Magda asked.

"Magda, every time you make a question like that, only makes me wonder, if you're questioning our love?" Guy said. *"What, was there an Art in your life?"*

"Guy?" Magda looked at him. *"I'm doubting, this is any about us."* She walked away.

"There, you've done it, Guy." Mona was front of him ready to go home.

"Glad someone enjoys the show, Mona." Guy said.

"Guy, this really doesn't have anything to do with you. Art and I have done all possible to leave you out of it. Except think, Desmon likes to take his place too?" Mona asked.

"Hm?" Guy looked at her. *"You know, when you girls like to laugh, with your friends, we guys taking life a bit to serious, when the heart? We tend to get heartbroken. Then, it's girls like Magda, too."* He looked at her. *"Was, I who decided to deny a past?"*

"Guy, between you and I, life about you and I, was over lots time ago?" Mona said. *"And to talk about it, wouldn't only mean, to hurt everyone else, around us, but, each other?"*

"Hm?" Guy looked at her. *"Just like you, Mona."* He walked away.

"Guy, has it happened, our past flushed back in your mind?" Mona was alone at the benches. *"And things, you never, knew?"*

"You just keep up with the show?" Art asked. *"Is it time to forget you have a real life, like a real heart."*

"Actor, you are." Mona tried to laugh. *"You know sometimes I get the feeling, that guy, still loves me?"*

"Ah?" Art watched Guy laugh with Magda.

"If they break up, it'll be a mistake." Mona said.

"Will it?" Art asked. *"Sometimes Mona, you don't mean to be selfish, just honest."*

"What do you know about, love, Art?" Mona smiled.

"Haha. I ask myself that all the time." Art laughed. *"Sometimes I feel like I still love you, Mona."*

"Oh, you mean, to cancel feelings out?" Mona asked.

Steps away…

"Guy, we could remain friends?" Magda asked. "We can get it right, this time?"

"Yeah, the girl I love, she's left me for my best friend?" Guy said.

"Guy, I only see Carol, with your best friend. You might want to find out who the real traitor is here?" Magda asked. "Because, it's not Art."

"Hm?" Guy looked at Magda.

"Guy, will life allow us be friends, after this is over?" Magda asked.

"Ah?" Guy and Magda looked at each other.

"Only means, we'll have to leave everything said and done." Guy said. "Talking like this, is it breakup, Magda?"

Steps away…

"Breakup on the ice?" Mona asked Art.

"Never the right place." Art and Mona walked out doors.

Back at Four Seasons of Memories. Would anything ever be the same?

"Boss, I've finished another project." Darla walked in Guy's office.

"Away at, any other office." Guy smiled taking the folder.

"Was, your plan." Darla asked.

"I, may try." Guy said. "Someday, I'd like to bring a girl to meetings with me. One that doesn't talk much. Knows when, one must."

"Guy, that's not an invitation for lunch business meetings?" Darla asked. "You'd have learned from business partners, quite well."

"Some business partners, looked for nothing more than, love. Ended up married." Guy explained business partners.

"I'm not interested, either way." Darla said. "Business, is what you made sure, you explained, about yourself and I?"

"Darla, if Magda wasn't in the office all the time, I'd call you with any excuse?" Guy said.

"Magda, without an excuse, but to make sure no girl is in your office, needs none." Darla said. "Not, that I notice, she's always in—" Darla tried to explain herself out conversation.

"Always in my office." Guy said. "We could spend hours reviewing this folder, all them?"

"Guy, don't give me the folders, just because—" Darla said.

"Have every excuse to see you at the end of the week." Guy admitted. "You won't come in my office, meetings, if I don't make sure to call you."

"We've become forbidden, Guy." Darla reminded.

"Darla, one mistake, wasn't enough, to realize, we're not one." Guy was front of her.

"I must get back to my office. Before Randy realizes, I'm not in it." Darla walked to the door.

"Darla, there's no reason with all that's happening, for you to run from me? Anymore." Guy did tell.

"Guy?" Darla hurriedly turned around. "All that's happening, what is it that's happening?"

"Hm?" Guy looked at her without an answer.

"You know, something about Randy, don't you?" Darla asked. "Yes, because if Magda was cheating, there'd be no reason for you to stay, silent about it?" She hurried out his office.

At Randy's office...

"Randy, Greg will be with friends, dinner." Giana said. "We could again, see each other?"

"Giana, we should stop seeing each other like this. This is all wrong." Randy walked to her.

"Wasn't wrong, to talk how close we used to be, when we were young." Giana said.

"Wasn't wrong for me to be here. Greg flirts lots at the office, always on the phone with some ex, feelings are still there for an ex?" Randy said. "Is wrong for that love, to have returned. Feels so right to have fallen back in love. Giana, we shouldn't be this close?" Randy asked.

"Why, not, Randy?" Giana cried. "You can't deny me forever?"

"Giana, don't make this any harder for me?" Randy asked.

"Randy, why make this love impossible for us?" Giana asked. "When we could be honest with them? Give into this love, *honest to ourselves? Talk about our day, like Greg with an ex. Isn't what's going on between us?"*

"Giana?" Randy said. "You're so good, at making me believe, it's that easy to give into, all this?" Randy kissed her.

At the door...

"Randy?" Darla whispered to herself. Tears roll down her face. "I trusted you?" She whispered. She wiped tears away, ran to her office.

"It's our past, everything. Just insisting we meet at every corner?" Giana cried. "I've tried, Randy, not to see you again?"

"I know." Randy said. "Impossible teenage love, wasn't over, we knew it."

"So, Randy? Will we tell them?" Giana asked.

"Will, I break Darla's heart?" Randy asked.

"Hm?" Giana turned away crossing her arms. "Feels like, no one else's heart matter, Randy." She turned looked at him again. "Doesn't mine?" She cried. "I love you, and all this is hurting me too. Stay away from you?"

"Greg. What about him?" Randy asked. "You go home, to ignore him completely?"

"That's only happened, well why explain, again? You don't believe me, do you? I don't exist in his world. Too busy with everything else?"

"I do, Giana. That's just the bad thing. You don't deserve to be put second to work, friends, an ex?" Randy said. "But, I'm not the guy to talk to. Greg, just might want to hear it, himself?"

"Forget it, Randy. It's not you between us. It'll still end." Giana walked out the office.

"Giana?" Randy walked to the door.

At Darla's office…

"Keeping busy with, something, Randy." Darla is alone in her office.

"Darla." Randy walked in her office. "Love you, babe." He kissed her at her desk.

"Randy." Darla walked to the center of her office. "Someday, I thought this was my world. I could hate something and wish it away. I could love something, ah, keep it close to me." She was front of blinds in her office. "Turns out, life brings you to your knees. You realize, you don't always, get what you want. Only, at times I feel, as if I never do."

"Guy boss now. Never was reason to bring him down." Randy looked at Guy's picture still blinds.

"My problem, Randy, isn't just an image on blinds." Darla said.

"What makes you say that?" Randy asked.

"I've just walked out your office, Randy. You've come running after me, as if you knew?" Darla said.

"Giana and I were, just—" Randy said.

"Friends since forever. I'd never known it. You've been in love." Darla said. "I don't blame you for it. Thought maybe, you'd escape every girl, you've known, met? Avoid it, at all costs, to keep me. The girl you've committed to. I thought, a ring meant more than, cheat?"

"Darla, allow me explain?" Randy asked. "Unless you're just looking for an excuse to leave me, run to Guy?"

"Guy is a married man, Randy." Darla said.

"That's never stopped you, Darla." Randy said.

"Randy, I make a choice, to be a better wife every day. We're not getting any younger. Someday, our own kids, will live through our lives. I'd like them to mirror themselves, without mistake?" Darla said.

"Our parents are nothing like us, Darla." Randy said. *"A new star in heaven, has been born."*

"I'd like that divorce." Darla said.

"Darla, don't give up on us, yet?" Randy asked.

"Maybe you never could forgive me, a past. Made a mistake. Love for Guy, a man who now belonged to someone. Life doesn't always give you what you want." Darla was front of Randy.

"You love me, Darla, don't deny it?" Randy asked.

"But, Giana." Darla said.

"Oh, forgive me? You've forgiven Guy?" Randy asked.

"This has all to do with us." Darla said. *"Correction. I'd like to know, will Giana divorce Greg, marry you?"*

"I was here to ask you forgive me, Darla." Giana was in the office. *"I tried to run from this love, from a past. I couldn't. But, Randy, if you want to marry me, I'll leave Greg?"*

"What, if I don't?" Randy asked. *"Because I'm still in love with Darla?"*

"Darla, if you allow, I make an honest question?" Giana asked. *"Darla has just told you, she wants the divorce. Will you be honest about how you feel, about me? Do you continue to be

in love with Darla? You've not told, I've not told. But this isn't the first time, we've been that close?"

"Ah?" Darla turned away.

"Giana?" Randy asked. "There was no need for you to—"

"Oh, Randy. I think both Darla and I deserve honest." Giana said. "It's the only thing I done, not, a tell? We could be honest, Randy? To ourselves?"

"Randy, Giana, may I?" Darla walked to her desk. "I must continue work?"

"Ah?" Randy and Giana looked at each other. They walked out the office.

"Randy?" Greg walked from Guy's office stopped front of them. "You, uhm, always get what you want, don't you?"

"Ah?" Giana and Randy turned around to look at Greg.

"Greg, I'm no player." Randy tried to explain. "When I give my heart away, I don't always have a backup plan. Already."

"Is that what it looks like, to you?" Greg asked front of Darla's door. "Giana, I thought I had finally found love. I was about to ask you to be, my wife. Though, wouldn't have worked. You'd gone cheating the same night, you'd married me. Real love, with Randy." Greg looked at Randy.

"I'm, sorry, Greg. How did you find out?" Giana asked.

"I saw Darla run out Randy's office crying." Greg said. "Once I peeked in the office, there was no reason for her to explain. Thought to give ourselves time, walked to Guy's office."

"You didn't tell him?" Randy asked. "Would only give him an excuse to come running to Darla's office."

"It's, just what I'm doing, Randy." Greg walked in Darla's office.

"Hm?" Giana held Randy's arm. "Randy, you aren't jealous? I mean, we've spent the night together? We've lived many moments around the office. Just think for a moment, all we've been. Lovers? You'll see, how Darla is just another beautiful girl in this company? It's I, you love, Randy?" She cried.

"Giana?" Randy was front of her. "Dinner, tonight?"

"Dinner tonight, Randy." Giana kissed him.

"Not what I'm thinking?" Guy asked side of them.

"No, we're in love, Guy." Giana was in the hallway with Randy.

"It's all right, Randy, truth about Giana and I, just rumors." Guy did explain.

"Guy, wouldn't make a difference to me." Randy said.

"Right, about Darla." Guy looked at his shoes with hands in pockets. "Now, there is more than history to that one."

"A ring, Randy." Giana cried.

In Darla's office...

"Darla, know this hurts." Greg said.

"Yes, you've been hurt by all this, just the same, Greg." Darla said.

"Thought the world was mine, to own." Darla said. "Turns out, the world may be stolen from you, every time?"

"Well, let's just remember, somethings, you just toss out your life?" Greg said.

"Ha?" Darla looked at him. "I'm sorry, Greg."

"Are you, Darla?" Greg didn't believe. "Don't, Darla." Greg looked down at his shoes. "Don't apologize, for love? Can't stress that one out enough."

"Greg, I—" Darla tried to apologize.

"Your book." Greg said. "Understood, every word. 'I never apologize for love.'"

"Greg, it wasn't about—" Darla said.

"You are doing nothing but apologizing, Darla. Way, I understood it." Greg turned to walk out the door.

"Greg?" Guy walked in the office at that moment. "Was talking with Randy and Giana. They're planning a wedding? Hate to break the news to you, both?"

"I'm sure, you do, Guy?" Greg was still front of him at the door.

"Greg, we've learned to respect each other, as the enemies, we've been?" Guy did try apologize.

"Thanks, boss." Greg walked out the office.

"Darla, maybe I could date someone else, forever?" Guy asked.

"You've divorced, Magda?" Darla asked.

"No. Magda realized, I'd never fall in love from you." Guy said. "She's divorced me."

"Guy?" Darla cried. *"Why date someone else, forever?"*

"You love, the impossible love, I am." Guy smiled front of her at her desk.

"I love you, Darla." He saw Darla allowed he run his hand through her hair.

...

"Ah?" Guy kissed her. Darla allowed him. *"At every meeting, every time we were close."* Guy said. *"I noticed you tremble, running away from this."*

"A mistake." Darla admitted.

"It's no mistake now." Guy said.

Blue Bay Hotel. A meeting...

"Art isn't about to walk in this office, is he?" Astrid asked.

"This is the meeting room, yes." Dario smiled. *"How is your marriage with Italiano? Has, Cobra finally confessed from a grave?"*

"I doubt, Cobra for one second would restrain himself." Astrid smiled. *"From, uhm, having himself called, calavera."*

"The skull." Dario smiled. *"Astrid, you were always innocent."*

"Did you know it?" Astrid asked.

"Why, Astrid, lie about it?" Dario couldn't understand. *"What made me believe your story all those years. Who really was behind that gun, pointing to Italiano's life? Not the romance, novel?"*

"We were both saving each other." Astrid explained. "I from allowing Reymundo find out, I loved Italiano, more, than he. Once I found out, all was true about Reymundo. He'd make a kill after kill. He'd sent Italiano to get killed. Every time I looked at him? I couldn't, Dario," She looked at Dario. "see, nothing else. I saw, crime. Looked in his eyes. I could no longer, say, I love you. Cobra. He had to prove his loyalty too. I could never understand, why Cobra allow I take the blame? Maybe, Reymundo would forgive me falling out of love, lots better? I had. It wasn't I who tried to kill Italiano, Cobra must? So, instead of allowing me, I make that kill, Cobra would. That way, if Reymundo someday found out, it wasn't I who pulled the trigger? Cobra would be found, a missed shot?"

"Ah? Worked." Dario said.

"Did." Astrid said. "Cobra knew, by killing Italiano, he'd have killed me too. I could never live without Italiano. I, we then did walk away guilt free. Reymundo never suspected, was his kill. I'd walked away from, that love?"

"Do you love him? More, than me?" Dario asked.

"Dario?" Astrid looked at him. "Allow, a woman continue be faithful?"

"Oh, but ask love to go away?" Dario asked. "Selfish I am, Astrid, moment you need me in your life, call me? I don't care who you are. I would love you just the same. Even when sinful."

"Dario?" Astrid looked at him. "Why live to cause tears?"

"Avoid them?" Dario with backward hand wiped Astrid's tears.

"Astrid, busy at your office?" Italiano is now in her office. "We've met at my office, Dario?"

"I've allowed myself the same respect for an office, as you, Italiano." Dario said. "Just wanted Astrid to know, you break her heart with, uhm, your ex-wife, I'll be near."

"Ah, but, a phone call away." Italiano said. "You'd like to forget business with me?"

"Hm." Dario smiled. "Might give me a reason to return?" He walked out the office.

"Astrid?" Italiano was front of her middle of the office. "You've ended your single life? I've forgiven you for?"

"Italiano, don't know what you're talking about?" Astrid turned away. "I, uhm, love you." She was front of him looking in his eyes.

"Astrid, don't mind you talking to your friends. Even dinner for some reason? But, will not forgive cheat?" Italiano reminded. "Let's be honest with each other?"

"Italiano, are we?" Astrid asked.

"Hm? How could you doubt me?" Italiano asked. "Not some novel? Our love?"

"I needed to hear it." Astrid said.

"I'm not blaming you for loving Dario. He was your husband at one point." Italiano said. "Love, is there already. But, don't you for one second forget, I love you. I'm, your husband now. Because, just the same, I'll remember I had an ex-wife? And there were feelings already born before—"

"I met you before?" Astrid reminded.

"Are you answering jealous?" Italiano smiled.

"I am." Astrid smiled. "Even when I'm bored at home alone. All I can think about is, you. Waiting to see you again, from the office. Sometimes, I think you're laughing with another at the office, and I get jealous. But right now, I'm in the office."

"Why I've come to see you." Italiano said.

"What was it?" Astrid asked.

"Dario this time?" Italiano said. "Was a good thing, I respected his time with you. He plays too much. One day, his joke has got to end."

"Italiano, you'll be gentlemen about it?" Astrid asked. "He's not crossed the line, with me?"

"You've seen it. Front of a lady, must be." Italiano said.

"Italiano, you are who, I believe you are?" Astrid asked. "You don't even smoke front of me? Criminal, just part of your undercover?"

"Hm?" Italiano looked down to a side. "Astrid?" Italiano held her arms. "Don't doubt me, for one second?"

"Italiano?" Astrid looked at his hands on her arms. "You're hurting me? But you, do know, that, right?"

"I'm sorry." Italiano turned away. "I hate you doubt me." He turned to look at her. "I allow, everyone know who needs to know, I walk by the law. Fine line? But hurts, when the person you most love, doubts who you are. Then, Astrid, how could you, love me?"

"If that's a question? Find out, I would love you, no matter who you are?" Astrid walked around front of him. "Hm?" She looked at him for a moment. "I'd love you even if you, weren't an act."

"Astrid?" Italiano got her arms again and kissed her.

"Italiano?" Astrid kissed him.

"Boss?" Lester walked in the office stood behind slightly to a side of Italiano. "Let's not forget, we're in the office. You might be caught, in love."

"Hm?" Italiano turned to a side. "I never do."

"Ah?" Astrid looked at Italiano. "Ah?" She looked at Lester.

"Astrid, I must get back to work. You, uhm, pretend work here. You might, not want to get caught. You go to jail, for it?" Italiano looked at her.

"Haha?" They laughed.

"I'll, uhm, remember that?" Astrid said.

"Boss?" Lester waited at the door.

"Let's go." Italiano walked pass Lester out the door to his office.

Italiano's office...

"You didn't let Astrid know anything?" Lester asked.

"There's nothing to, tell Astrid." Italiano is at his desk. He held a black pen in his hands.

"Maybe, Astrid is the kind that understands. Like a different man, so is a kill." Lester said. "While paperwork, a shot's fired a victim... While a courtroom, a shot has fired..."

"Can't save them all, Lester." Italiano said.

"One can only try, play god." Lester with hands behind him said.

"Was play?" Italiano said.

"Numbers, do they play, well?" Lester is behind Italiano's desk.

"When, a giant directs." Italiano closed a folder front of him.

"Hm." Lester had his hand on Italiano's shoulder.

"Thank you, Lester." Italiano said. "Can't trust many people, with a complete story. Your life."

"Won't." Lester said.

Guy and Sage are home...

"I'm tired of this, Guy." Sage turned to look at him in the living room. "First, we have to live through your parent's dream. Vacation, wedding, all?"

"I'm sorry, Sage?" Guy asked.

"Then, Nina, continues to be part of our lives?" Sage was front of him. "She's no act. No, she's very well real. And, you continue to talk to her, as if—"

"As if?" Guy asked.

"I want to know, right now, Guy. Do you love, the girl your own brother fell in love with? Let me know, right now. I will walk away, and allow you two be happy. Sure, Art will do the same thing?" Sage said. "Speaking of fair game?"

"Sage, Sage, please calm down?" Guy asked.

"Don't you make up any excuse, for me to calm down. You'd think, when my boyfriend is in love with his own brother's girl, is reason I calm down?" Sage explained.

"Not, his girl." Guy pointed out facts at Sage.

"Pretend nothing is going on?" Sage said. "How do you continue to be affected by, their lies? Cheating. They both should have told you, something was going on between them, the moment you, fell in love with Nina?"

"Maybe, like I knew truth, there was nothing going on between them?" Guy said.

"See, Guy?" Sage asked. "You tell me, you love me? There's no one else? Yet, you want to defend Nina."

"I'm not defending Nina. I'm just talking facts." Guy said.

"Why is it all about her, hurts you, when I'm right next to you? You should be caring about anyone? Than, I. If, Art's fallen in love with Nina, anyone else in this world?" Sage cried.

"Sage, I'm sorry, if I've offended you." Guy got a newspaper. "If, Nina and Art would talk wedding? Marry the next day, I'd be unaffected by it."

"Is that, so, Art?" Sage asked. "Because I'm ready to forgive you right now. Only, right now, neither, Art nor Nina are front of us?"

"Really, Sage." Guy put the newspaper down.

"Hm?" Sage turned away.

"Want Nina out our lives?" Sage walked away. "You'll do that?"

"Nina, has been part of our lives, since the moment she stole from our home?" Guy said.

"What?" Sage asked. "Nina stole from your, home?"

"It was at the cabin. Vacation home, Nina dare walk in and cry wolf for a first time. She was a kid?" Guy walked in the kitchen.

"What?" Sage followed Guy.

"Corbin thought, she was some hungry kid. Decided to call the cops on her. Cops came. Corbin never imagined, Nina would tell on him. He's sequestered her."

"Why would Corbin never, imagine a child would tell?" Sage, was she accusing?

"Because grandpa Corbin, never did steal her away." Guy said. "Art was behind at the hallway to a dining room. Saw it all. She'd walked in the cabin, at the time, we were on vacation."

"Does, Nina know all this? Because, no one's said anything?" Sage asked.

"Years, ago, forgotten faces. I mean, she has." Guy said. "With a child's fear?"

"Why would Art, quiet about it?" Sage asked. "It's Corbin, your grandpa?"

"Art was willing to tell on Nina?" Guy said. "Only, Corbin wasn't. Nina asked Corbin to give her money, all trouble would go away. Corbin said, Cops will never believe me, no one will, nor you. Nina answered, but you and I know the truth? I'm just hungry? But, ah, Corbin found out how hungry she was. She wasn't asking for lunch money."

"Why did Nina return to crime?" Sage asked.

"She wasn't the only hungry." Guy said. "She went ahead did it again. Art, had caught her again. This time he told, me?"

"You should have—" Sage said.

"Turned a hungry teenager in, that has no, parents?" Guy asked.

"She's got parents, just as criminal as she?" Sage accused.

"Sage, Nina is a changed woman." Guy said.

"I'll remind her, of, everything, everyone." Sage had plan in her eyes.

"Sage, trusting you with this story?" Guy said. "If Nina continued to be criminal, we'd turn her in, ourselves?"

"Why you must have given up on crime." Sage said. "Can't turn in, some people?"

"Maybe, not, when they've done more than lawyered up?" Guy said.

"What, else?" Sage asked.

"Cleaned up their act." Guy said.

In the living room before dinner...

"Nina, when you were a child do you remember? That cabin you walked in, crying wolf?" Sage asked.

"Sage?" Art who sat in the living room on the sofa reading a magazine stood up.

"Yes, Art?" Sage asked.

"Nothing?" Art was front of the girls.

"You know all about my life?" Nina sighed. "What is it, now, Sage? Corbin and Sherese decided to educate me, into a life without crime."

"Next to their own children." Sage said.

"Ah?" Nina looked at Art.

"Try to remember, it all best you can?" Sage asked. "That old man, wasn't alone in that cabin. Everyone was supposed to be out there, at the river. Only, not everyone was out there, picnic. No, one of them, was at the dining room's hallway, watching grandpa Corbin. Art?" Sage turned to look at him with a smile.

"Nina, we should stop talking now." Art pled. "Picnic, boat sail?"

"Why?" Nina asked Art.

"He doesn't want you to remember it." Sage said. "You might remember, an old, friend?" She looked at a photograph of a young family top of a chimney.

"Hm?" Nina walked to the photographs.

"Recognize anyone, Nina? A young man, still with hair." Sage asked.

"Nina?" Art pulled her arm making Nina look at him. "Can't continue talk, dinner time." He explained. "Sage?" He walked to the dining room.

"Nina?" Sage said.

"Hm?" Nina looked at Sage then at a picture of Corbin and Sherese with son Guy middle of them. He had a backpack.

"Corbin?" Nina saw. She turned to look at Art.

"I, uhm, ah—" Art was behind her.

"You, knew?" Nina turned around find him behind her. "You knew, all this time? I lied about Corbin, your grandpa? And said nothing? Why?"

"Hm?" Art shrugged. "Grandpa Corbin said nothing."

"Art, Nina, knew how hungry, you were. A child?" Sage said.

"Ha?" Nina cried looking down regretting.

"Nina, I would tell on you. I would. Only, grandpa didn't tell, and laughed because of a little girl crying wolf, for money?" Art said.

"Nina, maybe, you should leave. Before Corbin also remembers, it all. Not the child, not the young girl, you were, turns you in." Sage said.

"Ah?" Nina looked at Sage then at Art.

"Sage, you've not, told?" Guy walked in the living room. He saw everyone front of framed family pictures above fireplace.

"Ah?" Sage looked at Guy. "Maybe, you all should tell Corbin. Should turn her in."

"I remembered it all, the moment I saw Nina, at my doorstep, Sage." Corbin walked in the living room. "I was a young man, not a kid. Privileged, was no hungry person. I would never be looked the same, again. But, someone always knew exactly who I was." Corbin turned to look at Art.

"Hm?" Art looked down.

"Nina, and I knew who each were. A girl, would continue to be hungry. It was decent for her, to steal, but not to accept charity." Corbin said. "I decided, she'd have something to eat.

Besides Nina, wasn't the only who knew truth." He smiled at grandson Art. "Nina, also knew who I was. And, she was telling it."

"Hm?" Nina looked at him. "I'll be in trouble, with everyone. I would have never stepped foot in your family's home, yours, knowingly." She cried.

"What's going on, papa Corbin?" Guy walked in the living room.

"Nina—" Sage tried to say.

"Kids, you know how they are." Corbin walked to Guy with hug. They walked away to a dining room. "Sherese, dinner?" A voice is heard in the living room.

"Sage, you will keep a family story, I've trusted you with?" Guy asked his wife.

"I should leave?" Nina walked to the door.

"None sense." Sherese was at the door. "We have a guest for dinner?"

"Sherese wouldn't like to find out, why you're leaving, Nina?" Art asked.

"Why I'm leaving?" Nina said.

"Now I want to know why you're leaving?" Sherese asked.

"She's, uhm, enough family problems, Sherese." Sage joined them in a home's entrance hallway.

"Hm?" Sherese looked at Sage. "Sage, why don't we allow, Art and Nina resolve their problems, have dinner?"

"Yes, Sage?" Guy behind her asked. "Art, my brother, has lots to talk with Nina." He hugged his wife toward a dining room. "Hm?" He looked at Art. "Ah?" He looked at Nina.

"Ah?" Nina looked at him. "Hm?" She looked at Art.

"Dinner is being served, Corbin." Sherese followed to a dining room.

"I didn't want you to get in any more trouble, than walking into our vacation cabin." Art said. "So, I decided to stay quiet about you walking in our cabin, all on your own. Threatening, grandpa Corbin with some story, about he stealing you away, if he didn't give you the money, you asked for?"

"But, you'd allow someone lie about your grandpa?" Nina asked.

"You'd told the cops the truth, after Corbin had agreed about the money." Art said. "Hm, was feeling traitor, to grandpa, because I said nothing. And to cops. Had to pretend, I was still with the others, preparing that boat, for that swim? Was no picnic."

"Ha?" They laughed to a dining room.

"But they all knew, you weren't in that boat?" Nina said.

"Hm?" They all turned to look at Art and Nina at the dining room.

"Boat was big enough to get lost in?" Art shrugged. "But, I wasn't."

"Haha?" Art and Nina laughed.

"Join the table?" Sherese asked.

"I'm late." Blair walked in the dining room.

"Room for me?" Oso walked behind Blair to a table. "You know there always is, in this stomach?"

"Haha." They laughed.

"Never a full table." Corbin smiled.

"Haha." They laughed.

"Is it, uncle, Art?" Blair did ask.

"And family." Oso pulled a napkin unfold front of him.

After dinner left side of a home...

"What was the fight about, Guy?" Sherese and Guy conversed again in living space left side of a home.

"Nothing." Guy said. "Sage, just likes to exaggerate things."

"I, what?" Sage walked in the living room.

"You like, to exaggerate, things?" Guy looked at Sage as if in plead.

"Guy has fallen in love with Nina." Sage had cried to Sherese.

"Guy?" Sherese hugged Sage. "How could you?"

"No, wait, grandma Sherese. It's not what you're thinking?" Guy said.

"So, tell me?" Sherese walked to him.

"I didn't take my brother's girl from him?" Guy tried to explain walking away.

"Well, if it's your girl, you couldn't have." Sherese said.

"Only, I'm your girl." Sage agreed.

"Ah?" Guy turned around held Sage's hand. "About explanation? There was nothing going on between them, when I walked in the picture. So, I asked Nina to be my girlfriend?"

"Guy, I want truth?" Sherese asked.

"It's true." Art walked in the living room from his room. Staircase is steps right of that living space. "Never told Nina how I felt. She never told me, how she felt."

"You insist, about that?" Guy asked. "She hasn't told you anything, because she felt anything?"

"Guy?" Sage asked in a living room front setting. It faced away from a front home's window to a dining room and a fireplace.

"Art, if you marry," Guy looked at Sage. "Nina, I wouldn't care. As a matter of fact," He walked to Sherese. "I'd love for you two to be happy, together. That's if you are both in love with each other, and none of it, is nothing but, ha, fantasy?"

"Guy?" Sage sighed with cry.

"I mean it, Sage?" Guy walked over to her with hug. "I'm trying?"

"Try, harder?" Sage looked at him.

"Art?" Sherese walked over to grandson Art. They had their own conversation. "You and Nina, weren't seeing each other, before, Guy walked in that scene?"

"Truth is, no." Art said. "We looked at each other. I thought it meant something. Clearly, after brother Guy walked in Nina's home, I realized, it'd meant, nothing."

"Ah?" Sherese sighed. "I have nothing to worry about."

"Grandma, Sherese?" Art asked.

"Art?" Sherese held her heart. "You don't want to kill me with a heart attack?"

"Grandma?" They all tried to scold.

"It's just honest thing to say? But Nina, means nothing when family?" Sherese did say.

"Grandma Sherese?" Sage walked to them with Guy. "Guy and I would like to see family be happy. And if that means, Nina becoming part of this family, we'd both be happy about that?"

"I'm sure, Sage is being selfless about this. Just worried about a couple's happiness?" Art said. "Ours?" He looked at Sage.

"Art, I love you as the family you are to me. And I'd like you two to be happy. I know, what love is." Sage held Guys hand. "And since there's nothing between Guy and Nina, I see no reason why not do her part of this family?" She smiled at her husband.

"Hm? Making sure, a couple's love, remains uninterrupted. Ours?" Art looked at them.

"Art?" Sherese cried.

"I mean, if we'd be a couple?" Art corrected himself.

"Hm?" Nina walked in the living space from a living room right of the home. "I have a feeling, I've walked in the middle of family talk?"

"Nina?" Sage walked to hold Nina's hand. "It's about family, you."

"I don't understand?" Nina didn't trust Sage holding her hand. "What about?"

"Guy has decided to stop his act about how painful it is, to see you and Art together. He'd like you two, to be happy. And the only thing that will make you happy—" Sage said.

"Sage, we're front of Sherese." Nina pled.

"Nina both you and Art, have the right to be happy?" Sage insisted to Nina with cry. "Marry, Art? Being his wife, would make us," She nodded. "happy?" She squeezed her hand.

"Art?" Nina cried looking at Art.

"Art!" Sage cried with sigh. "I'm sorry, love does this to me. Makes me so happy? You've just made some kind of commitment, front of us. Family?"

"Love, for Guy. Must be." Nina said. "A single girl, may be decent."

"Nina, I don't understand?" Sage asked. "I'm but thinking of happiness, for both you."

"Sage?" Guy held her arm. "Enough? You've heard, marriage, their decision."

"Guy?" Sage cried. "I'd like that divorce?" She whispered to him.

"My brother, and Nina would like to discuss about this privately." Guy looked at Nina. "Love, is a private thing. We wouldn't want them to think we're forcing marriage?"

"Sometimes, people don't realize marriage, is a next step." Sage smiled.

"Hm?" Art and Nina looked at each other.

"Very, well, we'll allow they talk, alone?" Sherese smiled. "I'd like to be part of those, plans. Love?"

"But?" Art and Nina said.

"Mistakes, happen. We'd like to avoid it?" Sherese said. "Art and, Nina, you being apart, would be, one?" She looked at a married couple. Grandson Guy and Sage. She walked to a dining room with the couple.

"Art?" Nina cried.

"Think, we've understood?" Art turned away.

"What is it?" Nina asked. "Is it, you've hated the idea, of me becoming your wife?"

"I'm sorry?" Art hurried to turn around. "Have I hurt your feelings?"

"Ah?" Nina looked at him then to a dining room hallway.

"I didn't mean to. It's just that my brother?" Art said.

"Your brother means, more to you, than I?" Nina asked.

"Nina, he's brother?" Art asked.

"Hm?" Sage was in a dining room hallway.

"Hm?" Art looked at Sage. "I love you, Nina. More than my brother, besides the world?" He looked at Nina holding her arms.

"Then, are we, planning a wedding?" Nina looked at his hands on her arms.

"Hm?" Art and Sage looked at each other.

"Hm?" Sage walked to join a dining room.

"Art, are we planning a wedding?" Nina looked up at him.

"Ah?" Art took his hands from her arms. "I'd have liked to plan every bit of romance? But, uhm, we've fallen in love. Can't stay away from each other any longer?"

"Yes, of course, Art? Romance, is what this is?" Nina crossed her arms.

"Oh?" Sherese was middle front of them.

"Ah?" They looked at Sherese.

"Oh, we have celebration to plan?" Sherese must let everyone know.

"We've heard it." Guy with Sage walked in the living room.

"Who?" Guy and Darla walked in the living room.

"Nina, and Art, will be married?" Sherese put her hands together front of her on her chin.

"Nina?" Darla asked.

"Art?" Guy asked.

"Hm?" Darla and Guy looked at each other.

"Ah?" Guy son put his hands up front of him.

"Ah?" Sage turned to look at Guy son with cry. "I know, Guy, it's your brother. Of a life time?" She celebrated also with cry.

"Hm?" Guy son looked at Art.

"Hm?" Art looked at his brother.

"So, it's a done thing?" Guy son was front of his brother.

"Yes." Art answered.

"Nina?" Guy son turned to look at Nina. "You'll marry my brother." He tried to smile. "We've both found out, what kind of guy he is."

"Hm?" Everyone looked at Guy.

"You'll be a happy, girl." Guy son hugged her. "Congratulations."

"Hm?" They all watched them in hug.

"Art?" Guy son turned to look at his brother. "Congratulations. You both, deserve each other."

"Hm?" Art and Nina looked at each other.

"I can feel the love, already?" Sage smiled.

"Guy, trust your dad, a bit?" Guy hugged his son. "Once, you were on your way to an altar. You, made a promise, son. Of, love?"

"Let's save all this celebration, for Art. He's the one walking down that altar." Guy son looked at his father. "Making that promise. Of, Love, papa."

"I'm in time for celebration." Oso walked in the living room with Blair.

"I need a drink, taking your husband for one." Guy son walked out the house with Oso.

"What is it, we're celebrating, this time?" Oso asked Guy son.

"Wait till I, tell, you." Guy son walked out the door with his friend.

"Ah!" Oso closed the door behind him. "Ha?" His laugh is heard inside the home. "We've walked that, walk." He laughed.

"Hm?" Guy son got in Oso's truck. "Not on this side of the altar."

"Ha?" Oso saw cry? "Nina, she's uhm, been history?"

"When you need a drink?" Guy son and Oso drove away.

"A drink, it is." Oso obeyed directions. "Bull's bar, it is. Not trying to recognize your pain."

"Oh, not I." Guy son did laugh.

"Haha." They laughed.

Inside the home...

"What are we celebrating?" Blair asked.

"Art and Nina will be happy, married soon." Sage must tell.

"Ah? But you've never even dated? Have you?" Blair must ask.

"Ah?" Art looked at his sister Blair. "Surprise?"

"I am?" Blair must smile. "Congratulations." She hugged Art. "Nina, you sure about this?" She hugged her. "Family, you know?" She pulled her away still holding her arms with question look.

"Oh, don't be silly, Blair." Sage asked. "It's what we've all agreed to, bring her in. Family."

"Ah?" Nina looked at Sage.

*"Congratulations, Nina." Sage hugged her too. "Art."
She hugged her brother-in-law.*

*"Now, for that first date?" Sherese said. "Art, someday,
do tell about your dating?"*

*"Ah?" Art looked at grandma Sherese. "Was, no dating
at Imelda's home."*

"Oh, she's decent." Sherese smiled.

"Art, must you?" Nina asked.

*"Was, no act a fool. Guy has stepped back, allowed us,
be," Art said. "happy."*

*"Ah?" Sherese watched the new couple talk. "Hm?" She
smiled.*

*"Grandma Sherese, did ask?" Art said. "They'd all like to
know, it's real love?"*

*"Ah?" Nina looked around at a living room full with
family.*

*"Is it the grandkids? Congratulations, guys." Corbin
walked in the living room with hug. "Dinner, Sherese?" He
continued to the dining room.*

*"It'll be, celebrate dining." Sherese walked to a dining
room on left side of her home.*

"It is a celebration." Corbin smiled at the table.

"Ah?" Art pulled a chair for Nina.

"Ah?" Nina looked at the open chair for her.

*"Oh, love when you begin to date?" Sage said. "You just
wonder, if your boyfriend is really pulling out that chair," Sage
sat at the table. "for you?"*

"Hm?" Art smiled uneasy at Sage. "Girlfriend." He whispered to Nina.

"Boyfriend?" Nina also whispered.

"This must mean something?" Blair watched the happy couple.

"Ah?" Art and Nina watched them watching them.

"Grandma Imelda, will love this one?" Nina said.

"Must we," Art pulled a napkin from fold for Nina. "ruin the moment?"

"Thank, you." Nina took the napkin and put it on her lap.

"Ah?" Nina and Art, where they in trouble?

Create World...

"Our lives, are much like a story, Art." Guy is at Create World. "Precious Gems, belongs to Four Seasons of Memories. I'm willing to talk. Before you publish it."

"I've published, Precious Gems." Art said.

"I hate to go through this, with my best friend. Was." Guy admitted. "Business must be respected. I'll need you to honor that business. Not just partnership."

"I've signed a contract, with Mona. Can't work for two. Must remain faithful to one. Think, to remain friends, we might want to keep business part from friendship." Art asked.

"Business. Friends, you want to make business with." Guy said.

"Personal, I take it." Art turned on a match.

"You, changed much, don't remember you a smoke." Guy asked.

"Gene, and her bad habits." Art smiled. *"Now, they're also mine."*

"Parenting, is it?" Guy asked. *"Gene has ended up with Desmon. Afraid, Desmon is like father. Not easy to get serious, trust love, again?"*

"A town, like life. We share, one world." Art said. *"Ours."*

"Always did like my friends." Guy said. *"Right, and I yours. I date them."*

"Still, remember Verman wasn't the only who walked in Darla's office, asking for a job. Walked in her office, with a dress." Art said.

Years before...

"Darla, I heard you hire men with dresses?" Art in a dress and woman's voice walked in Darla's office.

"Must it be, they get more respect, that way?" Guy asked.

"Ah?" Darla looked at Art dressed as a girl. *"As boss, I've been impressed?"* She looked at him down and up. *"But, as you can see I'm in the middle of something?"* She gestured to Guy at the far right of her office. Her Desk is on the left, she was front of it.

"Ah, Guy this isn't what it looks like?" Art still with a woman talk, nervous as if caught held one side of his dress with one hand.

"I've known you for years, for me to believe, such act?" Guy looked at his friend.

"Hm! Hm!" Art cleared his throat. "I'll, ha?" He talked like a man. "Come back, in real attire?" He walked out.

"Didn't, quite work like it did for me, did it?" Verman was front of him in suit.

"Ah?" Art looked up at Verman. "Worked better for you, yes, it did." He walked to an elevator.

"We've gotta make a real impression." Verman held a folder in hands.

"Haha?" Men in working suits laughed in building ruin.

"Darla, do excuse my friend, Art. I assure you, I've tried? Art is really a tough act?" Guy is in the office with Darla.

"Ha?" Darla looked at Guy. "I try not apologizing for some friends. They mean their act?"

"Haha?" Guy laughed.

"Darla, has a suit, man's voice changed your mind, about that writing job?" Verman waited outside the office.

"Involves some bossing around?" Darla said.

"Not now, Verman." Guy closed a door.

"Darla." Verman said in his smooth voice.

"Haha." The men laughed moving office furniture around.

"Ah, guys serious about this job?" Verman said.

"Haha." They laughed.

"So, I try," Verman said. "be serious."

Inside the office...

"Want to start by dating, Darla?" Guy kissed her.

"Think we've kissed now." Darla smiled in the office.

Present time...

"Ha." Guy didn't laugh. "We like you better without, disguise. You turn in that Precious Gems, like it was produced, in Four Seasons of Memories. Ask, Mona to stop coming after all that's mine. About coming after what doesn't belong to her? Somethings, like time, you can't return, Art." He walked out his office.

Katie edits. Precious Gems presents...

Present time. King Art a man with mustache and beard walks in a meeting room of kings as queen...

"My King Lance?" Art in a dress joins a meeting of kings.

"Haha. Haha. Haha." Everyone in a meeting room laughs.

"Hm?" King Lance turns around and looks at all the kings. "Might we remind ourselves, kings we are?"

"Ha, hm?" The kings looked at each other quieting down.

"You've noticed I'm in disguise? One must to tell a story." Art dressed as queen walked in the castle and stood front of leading King Lance and the other kings.

"None sense, Art, once we've settled all this with the queen, you'll be king again." King Lance assured. "Now for

future threat? Must we figure out how to stop a war, with a king that's become, money...hungry? Without hurting, a kingdom's victims?"

"Once a king said, 'Can't really make an impression, freezing it, when other king has given it away?' So, the king, made instead an investment. Can't stay in disguise forever, so I'm out." Art slightly picked up his dress and walked out the Castle. "I do, apologize for my disguise?" Art turned around outside the office.

"Go ahead, King Art." King Lance said.

"Thank, you." Art walked away into a hallway.

"Is it Art is in disguised so one of us, traitor? Won't recognize him." King Randy said in King Lance's meeting. "One might get more respect, if he wore a dress?"

"Haha." They laughed.

"So, is there, anymore traitor?" King Lance, back in his castle asked.

"Ah?" Everyone looked at each other, without trust.

"We've returned now that, the queen has taken a crown back." King Lance said. "If only, to return it."

King Lance is trusted by all kings near by in a place called, A World Ruled By Kings. The Gypsies have no king. They've been known to make up their own rules and laws. Gypsies are asked to stay quiet, about dreams concerning the kings. But one Gypsy can't stay quiet about a dream, and comes to visit King Lance with it...

"Mom fell in love with a Gypsy man. But the king fell in love with her, asked her to deny being Gypsy, and marry him. She must deny being Gypsy, in order to marry that king." Tiska said. "She had two daughters. I've been told the reality of it, is she had two daughters. One still lives with her, but another was given away. You're not mother, Gypsy, so is it true, I'm the other of those two, girls?"

"I'm sorry, I can't stay and talk to you about this. I have to talk to King Lance." Gypsy said.

"Mom, but you've been asked, to stay away with your tell?" Tiska cried to mom Gypsy. "And, why is it, that Gypsy man Zuri, has called you in dreams? You fight with him about it, all the time?"

"Zuri has said, he's only tried to save me, from other gypsies?" Gypsy said. "And what about your friends? What is it, you look for, in that cave out there?"

"Ha?" Nothing." Tiska looked down. She looked at a photograph of grandpa on a wall.

"I've heard the king himself. King Lance asked I ask you to stay away from those caves, he thinks you're the ones that have been burning bushes, like rocks out there?" Gypsy was front of her.

"But, that's not us?" Tiska cried.

"You'll tell me, who that is, when I come back from seeing King Lance." Gypsy put her cloak and walked out her trailer home.

"Ah?" Tiska watched her walk out the door.

A town of Gypsies is dirt and some plants. Trailers is their community. Gypsy is on her way to the king's castle. She is on her way to the car that will take her to see the king, feet away. Rhett meets her on her way...

"Gypsy?" Rhett a man that frequents the Gypsy Town walked to her. "The king has fired me."

"Why?" Gypsy asked.

"I was late." Rhett said. "Know it wasn't the first time. But it wasn't my fault, my horse fell on its way there. Got hurt for a bit."

"Go find a job at another kingdom." Gypsy said. "With the war, no one has time to listen to my plead."

"Mine?" Rhett said. "I've begged."

"I have to get going." Gypsy moved a plant from her way. "That plan mixed the wrong way, might kill you. Don't eat it."

"I, won't." Rhett broke a piece and walked away.

"Ah?" Gypsy watched him cut a piece of a venomous plant.

Trailer homes are on land far from kingdoms at the right side. Land between kingdoms, and Gypsy town keep them distant. Zuri in Gypsy Town owns a Trailer home at the far-right end.

"Zuri, I'd like to move out of here. Everyone's got their own do, except for me?" Imani a Gypsy town's boy said.

"Deny your Gypsy, work for a king." Zuri a wise Gypsy said.

"You've heard about the dark cloud, no one wants to talk about. It wants A World Ruled By Kings." Imani said.

"They won't be in war for long." Zuri said.

"Meanwhile what do I do, bring that dark cloud, away?" Imani asked.

"So, when someone is coming after you, ask for the darkness to come protect you?" Zuri asked.

"But?" Imani asked. "Darkness?"

"Darkness can only be fought, with darkness?" Zuri turned away.

"So, I get it?" Imani said.

"Who is out there?" Zuri hurried to the door pushing it open and looked to the left and right.

"It's only me?" Micah a guy who'd pulled himself to the trailer in order to hide, had walked forward confessing. "I only wanted to know, what to do when I'm in danger, like Imani. Not that I believe any of it?" He shook his head.

"What, are you doing, following me?" Imani asked his friend.

"No, of course not." Micah denied.

"He's lying, he follows me everywhere." Imani told Zuri.

"Then you, Imani, should be more careful." Zuri said.

"What? Why? Micah is no danger. He's just some friend." Imani told.

"See, how I know who you are?" Zuri said. "Don't you go telling fibs, I'm Gypsy, boy?"

"You're afraid the king will shut you down?" Micah said still outside. "Why would you involve yourself with any of this?"

"I don't know?" Imani answered his friend.

"Know the king would ask we deny ourselves Gypsy, if he could?" Micah told his friend.

"Get lost, spy." Zuri asked Micah. "I see you around here again, I'm coming after you?"

"What for?" Micah asked.

"Cause, you're spying." Zuri reminded.

"Let's go to the caves?" Micah asked his friend inside the trailer home.

"I'm out." Imani walked out the home.

"Don't forget to call on the dark forces!" Zuri yelled.

"Did you let him know, we were only firing away fire?" Micah asked.

"He said, we could only fight fire, with fire?" Imani said.

"We, knew that." Micah said.

"I was hoping, his answer, was water?" Imani said.

"Hm? You say he keeps telling how, the answer to war, is travel?" Micah said. "I'm not going anywhere?"

"Not asking you to come with me. Find someone else to follow around." Imani said.

"Ha, traitor. You're leaving us, alone to fight those guys away?" Micah said.

"What makes you think they aren't part of the darkness. If they are, they will follow, me?" Imani worried asked.

"Ah?" Micah didn't have an answer.

In a cave to the left is a three feet by three feet round rock. Also three feet rock stand front of cave walls from one side to another. Light gives off from that walled rock. One bright light stands out at the left side of the cave.

"Don't tell anyone, who I am." A light sounds voice out.

"But, who are you?" Tiska is front of a light.

"Grandpa." A voice is heard again.

"Grandpa? Answer me? Why have you stopped talking? Is someone near?" Tiska didn't get an answer.

"Tiska?" Imani walked in the cave.

"Imani?" Tiska turned around.

"What is it you look for, in the caves?" Imani asked. "I know those lights are attracting."

"Nothing?" Tiska turned to look at Imani. "Why do you ask?"

"You come here, lots." Imani said.

"Imani, is leaving us like the traitor he is to fight those guys alone." Micah also walked in the cave.

"It might work, they'll follow me, to some kingdom?" Imani said.

"Mom Gypsy has asked we stay away from the caves. King Lance suspects us, the ones burning bushes and rocks." Tiska said.

"Let's just hope, their target is, bushes and rocks?" Micah cried.

"So, you leave right on time. Can't come here to the caves again. You really think, they will follow you, with their firing?" Tiska asked.

"Hm?" Imani looked at him.

"If you are here, we can fight it together. If you leave, you're on your own." Micah said.

"Hope, you're good and protected no matter where you are, Imani?" Tiska said.

"Hm?" Micah watched them talk.

"Ah?" Imani and Tiska looked at each other.

"You won't be leaving anyone behind, Micah. Love" Imani looked at his friend.

"No, cause I'm not going anywhere." Micah said.

Steps away at a cave entrance...

"Look at what we've found here? Some cave." Kimora hid behind a rock at an entrance.

"I believe, they've found this cave first." Averi said. "Let's fire them out of here?" He put his hands out to them.

"No, wait, this isn't an outside." Kimora held Averi's hands from firing fire out. "Let's go. Come back when they're gone." He and his friend sneaked out.

Steps inside the cave to the left, above the rock visible three friends talk...

"We fight fire, with water." Imani said.

"Contrary to all Gypsy Zuri has asked? Proving grown-ups aren't always, right?" Micah said. "Fight fire with fire."

"Can it be done?" Tiska asked. "Fight fire with water?"

"Haven't gotten water quite yet." Imani put his hands out to the light.

"What are you doing?" Tiska pushed his hands away.

"Worked, with the lights." Micah noticed the lights were now off.

"For, a bit." Imani saw the lights were on again.

"Hey, maybe Zuri had no idea, you could do water?" Micah said. "But you know, you leave Gypsy Town, you deny your Gypsy."

Back at Zuri's trailer home...

"Talking about dark forces, I've dreamed King Lance in danger." Gypsy was at his door step.

"They are kings, they are always in danger." Zuri walked back in his home.

"By the cloud that threatens kingdoms." Gypsy said.

"We thought it would spread." Zuri said. "How to stop it?"

"Your daughter Tiska, also would like to know, if she is really royalty?" Gypsy walked in the trailer.

"Well go ahead and tell her, she isn't before she believes anything different?" Zuri said. "Go ahead and ask her to deny it, before the king too, so she will have a chance at—"

"You know, Anya's heart is at no fault?" Gypsy said. "She fell in love." She turned away. "With a king. The king did love her, you've seen it?"

"Hm?" Zuri turned away. "Anya has taken it all."

"You allowed Anya be happy with the king. You remember it?" Gypsy said.

"Hm?" Zuri looked away. "What is it you've dreamed?"

"What, if the king isn't the only in trouble?" Gypsy asked. "What if, you along with the king is in trouble?"

"Why would I be in any trouble?" Zuri asked. "You're the one that's always helping a king. And it isn't always the right one?"

"Isn't?" Gypsy woman asked. "If it is, peace we ask for? You've been told, Gypsy we are, how we must ask for—"

"Peace. Ah, who believes in us Gypsies anymore? The kings ask we deny ourselves, fearful of us?" Zuri said.

"Must it be, that?" Gypsy asked. "When he's asked, we cover our face with our cloak?"

"What?" Zuri asked.

"When we are in any kingdom." Gypsy said. "King wants to make sure, we know; But a king. I've told him, he was in danger, about my dream? And, he saw it, threat."

"But he knows we would never?" Zuri worried.

"Well, if it is, we will understand how a king rules over us." Gypsy said.

"But?" Zuri looked at her. "We must tell this, to all?"

"All, but those who deny, being Gypsy, their Gypsy." Gypsy said.

Earlier that day...

"What is it, Gypsy? And know, you can't come in here with any of your tells?" King Lance said.

"See, I have no king to tell, this to." Gypsy said. "My king, a dark cloud appears above your kingdom?" She cried. "I know, I will be punished for telling you. But if not, to save your kingdom, and my people?"

"You go to your Gypsy people. You come around any kingdom, make sure your cloaks come down to your face." King Lance asked.

"But, my king?" Gypsy cried. "Why punish me, for telling truth? Allow, a gem save you?"

"There will be a gem, if you keep my kingdom safe." King Lance agreed.

"I will, my king." The Gypsy took a dark blue small cloth bag with a gem inside it from the king's servant. "Thank you, my king. Mix in a couple flower herbs, I'll do all I can?" She walked to the door.

"Gypsy?" King Lance called her back. "Why wasn't king Warren saved? If he asked and gave you a gem himself, with such wish?"

"Oh, but my king, one mustn't wish upon a star, with war, but for peace." Gypsy put her cloak down to her face and walked out the castle.

"Gypsies will keep their face covered, until, I ask they uncover." King Lance told his knight.

"My king, may I know why you've asked the Gypsy, keep their face covered?" Dario asked.

"Might they believe, they can do wrong on our kingdom? Gypsy, must know king." King Lance said.

"They shall, obey. Orders of a good king." Dario understood.

Months before. King Reymundo wants another kingdom. But his ambition has only begun…

"I want King Warren's kingdom." King Reymundo said. "And, after we have that kingdom, we will take another."

"My king, you can't fight King Warren. He's asked the witch Gypsy to take care of him." Knight Mitch said.

"She's no witch. She's Gypsy." King Reymundo knew. "So, have I. Asked Gypsy I win the war."

"My king why trust, a Gypsy?" Knight Mitch asked. "She works with the stars. She might fool you."

"But, a star, might never fool?" King Reymundo said.

"Very, well, my king. As you ask. We'll, die for you." Knight Mitch said.

"Oh, but you humble me." King Reymundo cried. "Who am I, so that you will die for me?"

"My king." Knights said.

"Your king." King Reymundo heard his loyal knights.

"Ah?" The knights looked at one another.

At King Warren's Castle…

"What is this knight doing in my office?" King Warren pointed at the knight.

"Ah?" His knights Ron and Roy looked at each other with a same question.

"We've taken over." Knight Mitch walked in the king's office. He put a sword through his heart.

"I've been killed by a knight." King Warren held to the knight looking in his eyes.

"Your crown, is now my king's." Knight Mitch looked at his men.

"Ah?" King Warren is on the floor front of his desk.

"My King Warren?" Knight Rylan knelt front of him.

"Serve, the good king?" King Warren asked on the ground of his castle.

"Ah? How will I know now, who the good king is?" Knight Rylan asked. "When threats have become, real?"

"Yes, my king, tell us who that king is?" Knight Ron asked.

"My king?" Roy watched him try to talk.

"Ha?" King Warren took a last breath.

"Ah? We were unable to save our king?" Knight Rylan stood in cry front of other knights.

"Looks, like we surrender to King Reymundo?" Some knights said.

"Looks, like you do." Knight Mitch said.

"You won't get away with this. This is a world ruled by kings." Rylan dare say.

"Meanwhile your new said king shows up," Knight Mitch said. "you will serve, your new King Reymundo."

"Hm?" Knights divided in same knight attire but different colors looked at each other in King Warren's office. Burgundy was the color of Warren's knights. Black is the color of Reymundo's Knights.

King Reymundo's Castle…

"A beginning of a story makes all the difference." King Reymundo said. "There once was, World Ruled By Kings. Then, I wanted more than I had. So, I began war, against Warren. A world of peace, was no more."

"Our world." Knight Dario was in his castle. "Aren't you afraid, now that we've known you a real war, my king, King Jakens will come after you?"

"When, a king after me, has fallen? Have I to begin another war? Will it be, against your King Jakens, knight Dario?" King Reymundo asked.

"A king after you? Has it, been the reason?" Knight Dario asked. "King Jakens does remind, 'When a king rises against one king? One has lost friendship, with all kings. Has brought them all an enemy, now.'"

"Sometimes, when kings come against, one king? Well, king one, has to come after a world." King Reymundo said.

"But you've just admitted, maybe those gems, worked in saving you against defense from King Warren's knights?" Knight Dario asked.

"Have they?" King Reymundo asked. "Those gems, also defended his castle?" He questioned. "Is what a Gypsy, said?"

"Gypsy, can't work magic, without a universe." Knight Dario said.

"Do, explain, magic?" King Reymundo asked.

"Gems, didn't keep your dark cloud from King Warren's kingdom? But, once you'd made your own wish? Was it Gems? Your life was granted, be saved?" Knight Dario said. "One, must ask for peace. Whole universe, will disagree about a won war?"

"You know, lots, Knight Dario." King Reymundo asked. "For I stand before you, talking."

"One must, before wishing on a star, king. Know lots." Knight Dario said. "A star's job is to take care of a world. Human must survive."

"Well, might this time, I not get what I want? Don't forget, King Warren came down, with my sword." King Reymundo admitted.

"Maybe, King Warren, unlike my King Jakens didn't wish upon a star?" Knight Dario looked at him. "Without warning? A waring king, like my King Jakens said, might someday be in the need of another's king faithful sword? A real war, arises? When the bad king has come after a world, with said defense, who then might you call?"

"Hm?" King Reymundo and Dario looked at each other.

...

"Dario, don't come around my kingdom, once a war has begun, with your king." King Reymundo said. "I've known a loyal, to your king."

"I'll, keep that in mind. Do remember, you've called me, but to be, messenger?" Knight Dario walked out a kingdom.

On blue beach waves. King Jakens' knight Art enjoys the beach. Knight Dario joins him...

"Love coming to the beach." Art a knight smiled.

"Art, taking that offer, from King Lance?" Dario also a knight asked.

"I'll have to." Knight Art smiled. "I'd like to someday, leave something for my kids."

"Kids will someday grow their own beans." Knight Dario smiled. "It'll grow bigger than our own."

"Ha?" Knight Art turned from beach waves to look at him. "I'd like to get a head start, in case things don't quite go as planned, with those seeds."

"Very well." Knight Dario said. "Know, I won't become part of it." He walked away.

"Looks as though, I'm alone in all this." Knight Art said. "Mom, was right? In life, sometimes you must stand alone."

King Jakens' Castle...

"Art, we're under attack. As, was King Warren." King Jakens said. "Think, we'll escape, not like King Warren?"

"I don't know. I'll do whatever I can, my king." Knight Art still looking at the king bowed his head.

"We'll need to be smart about this." King Jakens asked. "King Reymundo is a smart one, and he'll be making sure, he escapes, and with his kingdom. If he does, my life will continue in danger."

"Hm?" Knight Art thought.

"You may take knights?" King Jakens asked.

"You save, those knights, for a real war, my king." *Knight Art walked out the door. "Then, is it disaster, we must prepare for?"*

"Art!" King Jakens insisted about his knights.

"I think, if knight Art has denied, any men follow him, with your plan, my king... He knows what he's doing." Knight Dario smiled.

"Dario, a friend never abandons a friend." King Jakens said.

"Unless that friend, denies you join him." Knight Dario smiled.

"My king?" Imari walked in the office.

"Who's allowed you walk in?" Knight Dario asked.

"Imari, what are you doing here?" Micah walked in the office behind.

"He's brought a friend?" Knight Dario looked at King Jakens.

"There's no one at the door." Imari said.

"They'll be fired, again." Knight Dario said. "What is it you want, King Jakens is busy."

"I, would like, if I may? Work for the king?" Imari said.

"Why would the king hire you? Your friend Micah has followed you here, and you've not taken notice?" Dario asked.

"He did say, I'm a friend?" Micah said.

"Hm, ah?" Dario looked at King Jakens.

"You're hired." King Jakens looked at knight Dario. *"You will train, make sure they don't leave my door. Any door, I might be at?"*

"I will do just that." Imani said.

"What about me?" Micah asked.

"You, a friend has followed friend Imani, here. You're hired too." King Jakens said.

"Okay, my king, I'll train." Knight Dario walked out the office with them.

"Here, I am." Knight Rhett took a last step to side of door.

"He's just been hired. But you'll be in the kitchen now, Rhett." Knight Dario stood outside the door.

"Why?" Rhett asked.

"I believe, we both have a same interest?" Knight Dario said. *"Well, Knight Imari, Micah, now that we've resolved this problem, let's talk king's agenda."* He walked away with them.

"Where, were you, Rhett? I thought you needed an immediate job?" King Jakens walked out the door.

"I, uhm, visiting an old, friend?" Rhett said.

"You'll be working the kitchen now." King Jakens said.

"Why?" Rhett asked.

"Knight Dario has come up with a new plan. That saving my life? You've left my door." King Jakens walked back inside his office.

"The kitchen? The Kitchen?" Knight Rhett walked back and forth in the hallway. *"I hate, the kitchen? I'm a knight!"* He whispered in yell in place again.

At King Reymundo's kingdom...

"My king, you must have dinner." Emma a servant walked in his room.

"I'll be down in a bit." King Reymundo thanked.

"I'll wait for you, at the dinner table." Emma walked out his room to the right down a hallway, went downstairs, right a couple steps to an open dining room.

"King Reymundo, will be enjoying dinner?" Atia a servant asked.

"I'm ready for dinner." King Reymundo sat at the table.

"Very well." Emma walked with Atia to the kitchen. *"In this life, Atia, I'm boss."*

"You're welcome." Atia smiled in the kitchen.

In the dining room...

"I'm afraid, King Jakens isn't willing to give up. He'll come after me." King Reymundo said.

"I hope you're wrong." Queen Astrid said.

"I'm not, dear." King Reymundo held her hand at the table. *"I'll want you to get your things. Run to my best friend's castle, King Santino. He's agreed to take you in."*

"But?" Queen Astrid looked down at the plate front of her. *"I would never leave you. I'll die, with, you?"* She held his hand.

"Astrid, we've lived many lives. But it's come my time, for us to part?" King Reymundo took his hand from hers and looked down at his food.

"Hm?" Queen Astrid looked at him with cry. *"I don't understand? It's my own will, to die with you?"*

"Astrid!" King Reymundo didn't turn up to look at her. *"Am, I not your king?"* He turned to look at her.

"Yes, you're my king—" Queen Astrid said.

"Then, you'll do, as I ask." King Reymundo's conversing was over.

"Hm?" Queen Astrid turned away. *"Very, well. But you will find a way to survive, Reymundo. I'll run, as you've asked, to King Santino's castle. But you will come look for me, again."* She cried.

"Thank you." King Reymundo said.

"My king?" Queen Astrid asked.

"Yes?" King Reymundo turned to look at Astrid.

"Why, if you have much, want anymore?" Queen Astrid asked. *"If you loved me, you'd live a simplest life? Only to keep us alive, together?"*

"Someday, if all goes well, you'll understand why, Astrid." King Reymundo said. *"Life, doesn't remain the same, for everyone?"*

"But, my king?" Queen Astrid looked at him.

"There will be no more conversing about this?" King Reymundo pled.

"But—" Queen Astrid insisted.

"Please?" King Reymundo held her hand and kissed it.

"Very, well." Queen Astrid ate left side of him. He sat at the front of a table, front of a dining room.

Hours later. Art tries to make his way through trees and plants...

"Hm?" Knight Art turned back making sure no one followed him. "Ah?" He cuts plants away from his path.

"Where is it you're going?" Verman King Reymundo's knight asked front of cut down plants.

"Yeah, because if you're making your own path to King Reymundo's castle, you're going the wrong way." Knight Keen, Knight Verman's partner asked.

"Ah?" Knight Art was surprised. "You've caught me? But, finding out, exactly who I am? You'll see, you're really the ones that have been caught?"

"I don't understand?" Knight Verman said. "And I have a feeling, any other word you say, will matter the same. None."

"Wait a minute?" Knight Keen asked. "Allow, at least, he be funny with his tell? About how we are, in trouble?"

"I'm one of King Jakens' Knights." Knight Art said.

"Ooh, looks like he's right." Knight Verman said. "Being so, you might want to return. We won't turn you in. Being that your attempt to enter King Reymundo's kingdom, to play hero to King Jakens, has failed."

"Has it?" Knight Art asked.

"Has." They both answered offended.

"I, have found out exactly who you are." Knight Art said. "Allow me, the rest of, my story?" He put his hand on his shirt. "The king has offered me, a kingdom. If, I bring your king Reymundo down?"

"Haha?" Knight Verman laughed. "What makes you think, you'll do a sure thing. We've searched the area, and you come alone?"

"Haha." Knights Keen and Verman laughed.

"Ah? If, I do bring down such crown? A crown will be left without its king. It'll need one. King Jakens has offered me that, very crown?" Knight Art must believe. "Might not become king, as you have said, I'm alone. But, what if I do become king? Then, both you will be left out your own kingdom?"

"Ha? I think I'll bring down a want in king, before he steals my crown. It is up for grabs?" Knight Keen laughed.

"Ha? We might not want to continue with that laugh, Keen. You've heard, he'll keep us, if we be faithful, to a crownless king?" Knight Verman said.

"Ah?" Knight Keen looked at Knight Art.

"Hm?" Knight Art smiled at opposing knights.

Reymundo's Castle is a white castle. You may walk in two doors. Down three rounded stairs lead to a staircase straight ahead. Entrance is middle of a welcoming living space for guests. From one end to another is living comfort divided into sections with comfortable furniture, entertainment of some kind, as is a bar. Staircase has lots of room for many people to walk up and down at one time. Right of a white staircase is a dining area for gather of many people. Right in a dining room is *a hallway to a kitchen. Left to front of a kitchen is a tray held by both Emma and knight Art. King Reymundo and Queen Astrid wait in the dining room for dinner...*

"Still not gotten my last pay?" Rhett cried out the kitchen with a piece of bread.

"Please, allow, I take Queen Astrid, and King Reymundo, their dinner?" Knight Art asked pulling the tray from Emma.

"What is it?" Emma asked knight Art. "You've been too close to the king. I wonder why, that is?" she didn't let go of the tray.

"What is it, Emma?" Queen Astrid walked to them.

"Art has insisted, he take care of the king, closely. I don't trust him." Emma told still holding a platter knight Art held too.

"Art, I want to know what's going on? You wouldn't betray more than a man, who's accepted to take you into, his kingdom?" Queen Astrid looked at the platter being pulled.

"My queen?" Knight Art asked in the kitchen. A few words with you, alone?" He looked at Emma.

"Very well." Queen Astrid asked Emma.

"Hm, my queen?" Emma let the tray go. "Very, well." She walked out the kitchen.

"See, my queen?" Knight Art looked down at the tray of food as he talked to Queen Astrid.

"Hm, ah?" Queen Astrid listened. "What is it you're saying, Art?" She turned away.

"That, your king must go down, in order for my king, to live." Knight Art explained looking down at the tray again. "Your king, brings a kingdom down. While My king takes care of an

entire kingdom, himself, along with his queen. You don't want blood on your hands, my Queen?" He must remind.

"Art, that's your king? You said it, yourself, under that sword?" Queen Astrid reminded. "Your only duty, is not to question, but obey?"

"And, with that you've understood, I do, have a king?" Knight Art reminded of king Jakens. "Might you remember, why I do it? My own family, serves the king. Have in mind, if we could talk peace? We would, uhm, for our family sake? Turn in a crown, yours? For your own family?"

"I don't have anyone, but myself? I assure you. As enemies we, are?" Queen Astrid said.

"Save, yourself?" Knight Art holding the tray on one hand, held her hand.

"You, would, wouldn't you?" Queen Astrid moved his hand from his looking at the tray on his other hand.

"What is going on with my food, my wife?" King Reymundo walked in the kitchen from a dining room.

"My Queen, was just asking for dinner too." Knight Art had a tray with food in his hand.

"Very well." King Reymundo returned to the dining room with his wife.

"Hope this does nothing else," Knight Art served. "than make you feel better, my king?"

"Thank you, knight Art?" Queen Astrid looked at the king.

"Feeling better all ready." King Reymundo smiled.

"Ah?" Queen Astrid looked at Reymundo. "Hm." She smiled.

"Might we begin eating?" King Reymundo asked with hand on Queen Astrid's hand.

In the kitchen…

"I will not allow, you forget that's my king," Emma at the sink pointed toward the dining room. "in that dining room."

"What, have you forgotten, you serve a Queen too?" Knight Art asked.

"Hm?" Emma looked at plates in the sink.

"Don't turn away, Emma, have you?" Knight Art asked.

"It's my king Reymundo who's become Ill."" Emma reminded. "As you've joined a kingdom?"

"I simply hate my duties of knight." Knight Art said. "And, I've grown fund of my king."

"Why don't I believe you?" Emma questioned.

"Why, should I, believe you?" Knight Art asked. "Might we both want him dead?"

"Ah?" Emma looked at him. "Someone, knight Art, must stand for peace?"

"Ah?" Art questioned her. "Is that what you do here? Following, King Reymundo's orders?"

"I'm, a, cook?" Emma reminded with offend.

"Right, now you are. What happens when he asks you—" Knight Art asked.

"How have you escaped orders, ha?" Emma asked.

"They, enemy, have not come to the door, now, have they?" Knight Art looked to a kitchen's door, door to an outside feet right of a sink.

"Ah?" Emma looked at Art.

"Feel, much safer now, Emma?" Knight Art asked.

"What makes you think, I don't know sword?" Emma asked.

"Ah?" They looked at each other. *"I won't go down without a fight?"*

"Wait, are we talking war, against each other?" Knight Art asked.

"No?" They said. *"I'm no traitor?"*

"Against, a world?" Knight Art asked.

"Emma, knight Art, not sure who's in charge of a kitchen? But do take care of my king?" Queen Astrid walked to them at the sink.

"My queen?" Art asked.

"I've, uhm, accepted your worry for your queen, knight Art." Queen Astrid smiled. *"You've knelt, but loyalty?"*

"Ah?" Emma looked at Knight Art.

"Ah?" Knight Art looked at Emma. *"I, uhm, have."* Knight Art looked at Queen Astrid.

"Ah?" Emma front middle of them watched them talk.

Next day in a royal's room comfort. Queen Astrid must talk to King Reymundo...

"My king, you've asked, we not talk about it anymore. And I might leave, your castle. Believe there has been no betrayal, and that is just what I'm doing. It's been no betrayal?" Queen Astrid front of King Reymundo cried. "I love you, my king." She kissed him.

"I, love, you too, my queen." King Reymundo kissed her.

"Ah?" They looked at each other resting foreheads on each other in cry. They held hands front of them. "Haha?" They laughed.

"Are you ready? King Santino waits at his kingdom, for King Reymundo's wife Queen Astrid." Knight Keen waited for her at the door.

"I'm ready, Keen." Queen Astrid walked out the door.

"We've said our goodbyes." King Reymundo said. "As if, we'd never see each other again."

"She's taken all." Knight Art is in the king's room.

"She thinks, she has, Art." King Reymundo said in his room. "But, when all is gone, the kingdom, is ready with more. Then why allow my wife Queen Astrid...dirt on her crown?"

"Is that, it? About a Queen's crown?" Knight Art asked. "I was thinking you'd given up, on that war?"

"Not that, war. Has just begun." King Reymundo said.

"My king, if you forget that war, I'm sure King Jakens, will too?" Knight Art asked.

"King Jakens will turn in his crown, with all else, even his wife," King Reymundo said. "will serve a new king.

"Ah?" Art a knight, watched a king be king.

Days later...

"Tray, is ready." Emma smiled with a tray on a long center kitchen table.

"I'll help, with that." Knight Art took the tray.

"Art, I've prepared a tray, I will deliver a tray." Emma asked Knight Art give her the tray.

"I've only tried—" Knight Art let the tray go.

"I don't need your help, Art. You're a knight." Emma smiled walking out a kitchen.

...

"Art?" Emma walked back in the kitchen with a tray of food.

"You've insisted, on taking King Reymundo dinner?" Knight Art is in the kitchen with a glass of water.

"The king would like you," Emma was front of knight Art. "take him the food personally. He's become ill, in his bed. And doesn't trust but you, Art?" She wasn't happy.

"Very well." Knight Art took the prepared tray.

"Art, mustn't we ask for peace?" Emma gestured fist plead with hand front of her.

"Has one, Emma, a chance?" Knight Art held his step and continued on his way toward the door to a hallway.

"Ah?" Emma watched knight Art walk out a kitchen. A long wood preparation table is middle section of a kitchen.

Sections to store food at the top and bottom, with breads, fruits, other foods center at a four-wall kitchen. A sink at the left side, of a kitchen says it's a front's kitchen, under a window out to garden of herbs and foods.

In King Reymundo's bedroom...

"Art, I know you've come for some reason. Since the moment you came, I've become ill. In bed now. Do, what you will." King Reymundo said. "Knowing I've given you my trust, over everyone else."

"My, king?" Knight Art at the door continued his way to the bed. "You'll see, with this food, you'll be up and serving as, a king must. Let it be, I'm not a curse, but a blessing." He put food at his bed. "Sometimes, one must save," He told. "a world."

"Thank you, Art. I knew, if anyone, wouldn't be you." King Reymundo ate.

Moments later. Outside the door...

"Emma, keeping watch, for a king?" Knight Art walking out the room was surprised to find Emma next to the door at the left.

"Thank you. Least you could do, is allow I keep a watch, right outside my king's door." Emma waited outside King Reymundo's room.

"It's all. Been taken care of." Knight Art must say.

"Art?" Emma in cry understanding knight Art's words held hands in fist. "My king?" She ran in the room.

"Hm?" Knight Art stood outside the door. "We might want to evacuate."

"We'll need to take him down, as one's king deserves?" Knight Keen had walked upstairs with knight Verman.

"Knights will wait, at every other step of a staircase. Swords pointed down next to feet, top part of sword pulled forward front of every knight." Knight Verman asked.

"Meanwhile, a king will come downstairs from his royal room, out his castle for a last time." Knight Keen said.

"Very well. We continue to play, kingdom." Knight Art at stair hallway front of them said.

A doctor is in the room, and out a room. He is right. King Reymundo has been poisoned with his food. Downstairs everyone waits to watch a king who's lost a kingdom, his crown be taken out a castle...

"There has been a traitor!" Rhett hurried in the castle. *"King Reymundo, has found out, what it means to lose it all!"*

"What is it, you're saying, and why?" A man part of a kingdom's crowd asked.

"Once, the king threw me out his kingdom." Rhett told. *"I was left in the cold, to die?"*

"But, you didn't?" The man reminded.

"If it wasn't for another man's kingdom." Rhett said.

"Make way, for a once king?" Knight Keen asked holding the king on a bed with others.

"And we are out." Mitch a last knight at stairs put his sword back in place and followed the other knights out the castle.

"Who was traitor?" A man asked.

"Which among us, poisoned the king?" Another man asked.

"Well, king Art, will you confess, yourself a traitor?" Emma asked in the crowd.

"We might want to get out of here!" Knight Art asked. "This castle like his king is about to be brought down!"

"Ah!" Everyone ran out the castle after a king who was brought out.

"Art, why aren't you running out the castle?" Emma asked. "Like everyone else?"

"Why aren't you?" Knight Art asked.

"Ah?" They looked at each other.

"Not the moment for romance?" A Knight ran back inside the castle.

"Emma, run?" Knight Art held her hand pulling her out castle doors.

"I think he's serious?" Knight Verman followed out the castle.

"Ah?" Knights looked at each other and ran out the castle.

"And a real kingdom, might live!" Knight Dario yelled with command front lined knights.

Half of a castle is in ruins.

"We've lost our king." Everyone knew why.

"Who will be our king? We need a king?" Everyone watched King Jakens' knights leave.

"All kings must agree." A kingdom knew.

Day's before at king Santino's castle...

"My queen, king Reymundo has asked, I allow you find safety in my kingdom. But allow, I offer you my home, as your own?" King Santino kissed her hand welcoming Queen Astrid to his castle.

"Thank you, my king?" Queen Astrid smiled.

"If you need anything, my queen, I will do whatever it takes, to please you." King Santino smiled.

"You've, been that kind of king. I have no doubt, I could not be any better, at any other, home." Queen Astrid smiled.

"Makes me feel lots better to leave you, to the king." Knight Keen walked out the castle.

"I ask we be quiet about, this?" Queen Astrid asked.

"But, might a heart, quiet love?" King Santino said.

"Oh, but is it love, when Reymundo's Queen?" Queen Astrid did remind.

"I'll quiet my love for the queen, as you've asked." King Santino turned away. "Forever."

"You won't bore here, my queen." A servant assured.

Present time. Queen Astrid has stayed in the castle for days. Knight Keen visits her, with news of King Reymundo...

"My queen, your King Reymundo has left us." Knight Keen walked in the castle.

"My queen?" King Santino, who is in the living room with her, walks to her. *"I'll be right here for you, my queen?"* He held her hands.

"My king?" Astrid looked at him in cry.

"Hm?" Knight Keen looks at them who look at each other. *"My king waits for me."*

"Your, king?" Queen Astrid turned to ask.

"King Jakens has made knight Art, a traitor, king with a lost crown. But, then again, you knew that, my queen?" Knight Keen dare accuse.

"Hm?" Queen Astrid hurried to look at King Santino with deny.

"Hm?" King Santino looked at her with trust. *"The queen is not well, with your news. Might you, find your kingdom?"*

"Very, well, King Santino." Knight Keen walked out the home.

"Is it, you will accept my love?" King Santino held her hands.

"And quiet about it?" Queen Astrid turned around. *"I've just become widow."* She cried.

"My Queen, allow I be here for you?" King Santino walked to her and held her arms from behind.

Knight Art must talk with King Jakens. Is it true, he will be crowned king?

"The king is gone." Knight Art is in King Jakens castle. "But my king, is it that I'm guilty? Traitor? To have asked the king escape with his Queen Astrid?"

"You now have your kingdom, King Art, your own crown." King Jakens said. "I've made sure, that castle, was brought down."

"It survived some. Because, I was in there." Knight Art asked.

"Only way you will become king, is you go up to that king's room. Take that crown out that crystal box and put it on...front your people." King Jakens said. "Only way, your people will recognize you, as their new king."

"My king, but that is nearly impossible? Knights Keen, and Verman are in for that crown, too." Knight Art said.

"Then, you might want to run, for that crown." King Jakens said.

"I, will." Knight Art hurried to the door.

"King Art?" King Jakens asked.

"Yes?" Knight Art turned from the door.

"You'll make a good king." King Jakens said.

"Thank you." Knight Art continued out the door.

At castle half in ruins. A crown sits inside a crystal box on top of a pillar left of a royal bed...

"You said, you wanted to tell me something. Kings had agreed, how someone may take possession as king of this lost kingdom?" Knight Verman asked.

"The only way, anyone will take over this kingdom," Knight Keen said in a living area in the castle. *"is we find that crown, and wear it front of everyone. This kingdom."*

"You've found out?" Knight Art is back in the castle.

"Ah!" They all ran upstairs for the crown.

"It's in the king's bedroom!" Knight Art ran in the room.

"It's survived." Knight Keen cried also in the room.

"Go ahead and call in all the kingdom, for we've found our new king?" Knight Verman also in the room cried a lost crown.

"Don't worry, Verman, you're not the only who's lost that crown." Knight Keen said.

"I'd be a better king." Knight Verman said.

"Thanks, for understanding, guys." Knight Art had reached the crown first. He held it in his hands. *"Hm?"* He raised it front of him above his head.

"Ah?" Knights Keen and Verman worried he'd put it on, they have lost it.

"I'll wait." Knight Art held it in hands.

"Hm?" Knights keen and Verman worried looked at each other.

"Suppose, I take it during his sleep?" Knight Keen asked.

"Suppose, I'm not part of a lie?" Knight Verman said.

"Keeping something important from the king, such as his own death, is betrayal." Knight Keen reminded.

"Suppose, we both kept that from the king?" Knight Verman asked. *"Besides, a crown is only real, when a real king wears it."*

"So, what do we do with this one?" Knight Keen asked.

"We, uhm, serve him. Meanwhile, his crown is taken from his head." Knight Verman said.

"Suppose, the whole kingdom, recognizes him as king?" Knight Keen asked. *"What do we do then? They'll bring him, gifts. He won't need, anything?"*

"I suppose?" Knight Verman said. *"We've become real gentleman, then?"*

"Ah?" Knights Keen and Verman dreamed.

"Don't you even think of it? Take my crown." Knight Art held his crown. *"You'll awake, an entire kingdom, mine."*

"Hm?" The knights looked at each other. *"Ah?"* They looked at, a king?

Next day a crown must be worn. A stage is set outside front left side of a castle. A king must be named...

"And, I name myself, as all have agreed, King Art." Knight Art put a crown on his head front of a kingdom, making himself new king.

"Ah!" Everyone cheered. They had a new king.

Inside a castle...

"And now, my king, a gift." Knight Keen said.

"For, accepting to become, our king." Knight Verman allowed one person at a time, to present King Art with, a gift.

"Thank you." King Art thanked. "Thank you…." A king received one gift and another. He watched baskets and more gifts fill a castle's living space.

"No one can deny him king anymore. Not with all their treasures." Knight Verman said.

"They've not only accepted, but welcomed new king." Knight Keen said.

Later that day…

"Do send them my appreciation?" King Art asked his knights.

"Will." Knights agreed inside a castle.

"My king, when will these ruins look like a castle again," Knight Keen asked. "and take our place, as your trusted men?"

"When, I've made a complete staff hire." King Art said.

"King, you have crowned yourself, King Art." Emma was in the castle.

"Emma?" King Art with smile welcomed.

"I've decided to investigate, King Reymundo. With it, I've ended up investigating you. Though, looks like phase two of my investigation, has become war." Emma said.

"That explains, your attire?" King Art saw she was a knight. "You could work for me, you won't have to, uhm, kill anyone?"

"You have, king." Emma knew.

"Only, under the order of my king, was." King Art said. *"I assure you, without an order, I'm not threat. Then, again, am my own king now."*

"New king, does come with new enemies?" Knight Keen agreed.

"Now, why would that kind of king, be crowned?" Knight Verman asked. *"Peace is, we look for?"*

"I will put even you, king, behind bars. Soon as I have something against you." Emma said.

"Like what?" King Art asked. *"I've already told you, it was under a king's order."*

"And, I will confirm that." Emma said. *"Still, king, you have a crown on your head."*

"Hm, this?" King Art took it off.

"Ah?" Both King Art's knights looked at him with worry.

"Ah?" King Art put the crown back on. *"Were you both coming at me, without a crown?"* He asked.

"Hm?" Emma looked at the knights.

"We had question about you, Emma?" Knight Keen said.

"And, I?" King Art said.

"And, I about you." Emma said. *"I'll come back, when I've gathered enough evidence. Hope it's not handcuffs, I'll be needing."*

"An apology?" King Art asked taking off the crown.

"Ah, you might want to keep that crown on, while we investigate?" Emma walked out the castle.

"Emma?" King Art asked. "Would you like to join me for dinner. See, new king, I don't have many friends, I can trust?"

"You know, I'm investigating you?" Emma said.

"I could say," King Art walked with her to the dining room. "same thing."

"Investigating me, for what?" Emma asked.

"I, don't know." King Art said. "I'm king, would only be fair, I investigate before you walk back in my castle? May I ask, why you've accepted to have dinner with me?"

"I'm hungry?" Emma said. "Like you don't know, I'd take any opportunity, to—"

"Investigate you, boss." Knight Keen stood at the table front of them.

"Can't just steal a crown like that, King Art." Emma had dinner with the king.

"I, uhm, might have an excuse for it?" King Art said.

"What? Ambition? Riches, in your mind? Wearing them on your head, doesn't make anyone king. To be king, you must—" Emma said.

"What, tells who a king is, Emma? Would you like to rule the world, with me?" King Art held her hand.

"King Art?" Emma looked at his hand on hers. "Does a king, rule, like this?"

"Ah?" King Art took his hand from Emma's. "I'm sorry, Emma. The time we've spent together, in this very castle?"

"Remind yourself. We were paid to work here, together?" Emma asked.

"Both, as traitors, to this castle." King Art did remind.

"But does a traitor not continue to rule, under his new king's orders?" Emma questioned King Art. "Hm?" She looked at the knights who waited at their table at the right end of the dining room hallway to kitchen. Table extends front to end of a dining room. They sit front of a dining room. Open dining room is front of right-side rounded staircase.

"Hm?" Knights Verman and Keen looked at her also without answer.

"Well, King Art, may I know, how you plan to rule your kingdom? If not by the same hand of an old king? Your, king?" Emma asked.

"Hm, ah?" King Art looked at her.

"Ha?" Emma did ask for answer.

"Hope, the fact you're having dinner with me, hasn't ruined your appetite." King Art ate in company.

"I don't know what to make of you, my king. Was, a couple weeks you worked for King Reymundo, gaining his trust. Yeah, all know you a traitor?"

"Hm?" Knight Keen and Verman cleared their throats. Was it, denial? Was it, they themselves are traitor? "Hm?" Knight Verman and knight Keen smiled at each other.

"No sense in—" Knight Verman said.

"No, no more sense in confessing, anymore." Knight Keen agreed.

"Hm. Who is it, you work for, Emma. You yet to tell?" King art drank from his glass.

"My queen, she will own all that has been taken, unlawful." Emma admitted.

"Ah." King Art and knights sighed.

"Who did you, think, I worked for?" Emma asked.

"There, is Queen Astrid." King Art explained.

Days later...

"And, I've said, I would be your king." King Art said.

"We thought, that meant, we'd be more than your servant." Keen said.

"You're not knights." King Art said. *"I will need you to be faithful. See, I'm not one to look for treasure, while a war. But, peace?"*

"What is it we do, here on the beach?" Keen asked.

"I've always loved to walk on beach sand. What is it, that's going on over there?" King Art looked to ocean water toward a boat.

"Where?" Keen and Verman walked closer to beach waves. *"It's one of King Randy's ships. It's under attack. He won't like this."*

"How can you tell, it's under attack?" Verman asked.

On water a ship...

"King Randy must give in." Guy one of King Santino's Knights threw himself with roll onto the boat.

"Haha?" Greg one of King Randy's men laughed watching him fall onto the boat. "Why haven't you invited Guy, a king's knight in your boat? He's had to throw himself in?"

"I have no idea?" Captain Zen said.

"I'm taking your boat for one of my own." Knight Guy stood up.

"Why, should I give in?" Captain Zen asked. "It belongs to King Randy."

"Why don't you go for a swim?" Captain Zen threw one of his men off the ship.

"Ah!" The man was thrown off a ship.

"Why have you done that?" Knight Guy asked. "We've come for a swim, that's all. Is it you've sent for help from your king?"

"No, I've asked he come with food, for a king's knight?" Captain Zen assured.

"I don't need, anything special. I'll have whatever, you're having." Knight Guy sat at a table.

"Ah, was ready for dinner?" Captain Zen sat at the table. "Well, you've heard, he's hungry?" He looked at his men standing around.

"Very well." They all hurried to continue serving food as it had been interrupted.

"Ah?" Knight Guy looked at his plate. It was empty. "I must say, no idea what you've put in the food. But it's invited me back to my ship?"

"Hm?" They all looked at each other and the captain.

"I assure you, it's the same thing, I've had. Maybe, just a bit more spice, for a knight?" Captain Zen said.

"Hm? Very funny. Yes, of course, you must take care of the king's ship." Knight Guy said.

"I believe, you've been warned? If one king dare come against another, it loses friendship with all others." A captain said.

"Remind yourself, you are captain." Knight Guy asked.

"King Reymundo made a mistake. Don't you make one?" Captain Zen asked.

"Prepare my boat, I'm going down?" Knight Guy yelled to his men below.

"Ready, Guy." A man yelled up to him from a small boat.

"I have no idea what, his name is?" Knight Guy looked at the guy who helped him back in the small boat. "One of my queen's men."

"I will see you, no more?" Captain Zen asked above from his ship.

"Perhaps you will, a king's place is, the world." Knight Guy sailed away.

On land...

"Well the king's knight has come down to his ship. But how did you know, the other was pushed off the boat?" Keen asked.

"People, when taking a swim, don't spread legs and hands." King Art said now, in King Randy's castle. "They, usually go hands in dive, into water."

"Why would King Santino, want to come after my kingdom?" King Randy asked.

"He's just like his friend Reymundo." King Art said. *"Wasn't faithful to his own best friend."*

"What is it, you're saying?" King Randy asked.

"Never mind that." King Art said.

"Why is it, you've betrayed King Santino, allowed I find out, he's after me?" King Randy asked.

"I'd like a same loyalty." King Art smiled. *"Of course, if King Santino asks, I've only come meet, another meeting with you. Not, interrupted a message, I've found myself on sea?"*

"With confirmation." King Randy said. *"Why, when you've heard the rumored about me?"*

"Let's say, rumors have been, but that?" King Art smiled.

"Right, he might think, if you'd chosen a side, would be, mine?" King Randy asked.

"A king, though part of A World Ruled By Kings, might he rule, alone?" King Art asked.

"A crown that owns, none." King Randy understood. *"But now with this, I've become in debt to you."*

At King Santino's home...

"Why is it, you've looked for war?" Queen Astrid turned away. *"I ran from a king, who wanted war for treasure, and you ask for the same?"*

"My queen, once you've seen all I may offer you, you'll see, friend King Reymundo couldn't give you, nearly what I will?" King Santino said.

"But, it's not riches, I look for, but your love?" Queen Astrid cried.

"I will prove, I'm not Reymundo's failed plan to rule the world?" King Santino said.

"But false, pride?" Queen Astrid turned away. "You know I may own anything I want." She turned to look at him.

"Do you know, what is offered to royalty, like that?" King Santino asked.

"King Randy isn't one to toy with?" Queen Astrid cried.

"I know you're afraid for me, I assure you with my men alone, there's no reason for it." King Santino said.

"Don't you dare involve my men in your...that business?" Queen Astrid said.

"I'm afraid the moment they've stepped in this kingdom, they've become kingdom." King Santino said.

King Art continues talks with King Randy...

"King Randy, why fight King Santino? You his friend, were there when king Reymundo lost his crown." King Art Asked.

"They were closer friends?" King Randy said.

"Ah." Art tried to understand kings' friendship. "You're invited to every one of his parties? Surely losing any more of your men, isn't worth this, war?"

"King Art, I have something to prove." King Randy said. "Once, I've come after Santino, he'll understand, who's king. Not, Reymundo, nor his friend King Santino's failed plan to take my crown, will do what I will. See, I'm not only seeking revenge for King Santino's bad humor to come after my own crown—"

"Then, what is it, King Randy?" King Art hurried to ask.

"After, I take King Santino's crown, I will come after yours. And, every other crown that World Ruled By Kings owns." King Randy said. "I will take all crowns, make it one."

"But you've heard the kings. You'll be alone to fight all crowns. Once you've looked for one crown, for no reason at all?" King Art said. "I've just joined crowned kings, and I've heard it myself? Have you no fear? We all come after you, for that one crown, you plan on taking, first?"

"Ah, but one must care for one's own crown. Save, it all for their own war." King Randy said. "You don't think, I'll play big brother and come fighting, a king? If it's not my own war, yet?"

"Ah?" King Art looked at him. "Hm?" He looked down to a side.

"War, King Art, isn't an easy thing. One must make wise decisions." King Randy said. "I had prolonged coming after every crown. When I got King Santino's knights knocking at my door, for my crown. Crown for their king?" He was insulted.

"What you do know now. King Santino. Is he after your crown?" King Art questioned.

"I am." King Santino walked in the kingdom's office. "And, I will have it."

"You will not, have, not my crown." King Randy a tall man is front of him. "To have it, is to die."

"But, I'm serious, you will lose your crown to me." King Santino looked up at him.

"Suppose, my men are as strong as I am?" King Randy looked down at him.

"Maybe, I should think about it, before I come after anything else that belongs to you?" King Santino said.

"May I know, why you've changed your mind about it?" King Randy asked.

"You and I, both have been warned and by your own men." King Santino looked at King Art. "And others. One can't fight a war like that. They've called it, greed. Senseless war."

"I assure you, advised not? I still win war, against you." King Randy said. "You've, started something. And I plan on finishing it. I had plans of it, for later. World Ruled By Kings. Taking every crown for myself. But since you've started, a war, my plan has been begun."

"King Randy, forget it all?" King Santino asked. "I will not war against you, I've told you."

"I still want to own the world." King Randy said. "I will come after every crown, there is."

"Hm?" King Art and King Santino looked at each other.

"And, so we've agreed on putting down the swords?" King Art asked middle of them.

"We'll have to call a meeting, with King Lance. Maybe, then you'll see some talks, aren't just talk. You've come looking

for trouble now." King Santino said. "Wouldn't be fair, I leave without reminder of who every crown, is, my King."

"Exactly, my point, King Santino." King Randy was front of him.

"Hm?" King Art middle front of them watched them talk. "King Lance one, we kings run to with our problems. But, we've not had reason to bother a busy king, with real troubles?"

"I was here to invite you to a celebration. Forget the whole, incident?" King Santino said.

"May one forget, after we've been...let's say? Boarded?" King Randy asked.

"It is wise, a king rectify." King Santino said.

A world ruled by kings. One kingdom King Reymundo's is middle of two more kingdoms top and three more below it. Two above are; First kingdom mountain top right side belongs to King Santino, it's mostly forest. Far right neighbor kingdom is King Randy's Kingdom. King Jakens below Reymundo's kingdom in right side at ocean. Also a middle kingdom, to the right King Warren's Kingdom. King Lance is neighbor to the far right of King Warren's kingdom. His kingdom is a bigger from all six kingdoms. He calls kings' meetings, when in trouble. There is little argument when a problem. But meetings haven't been, an easy one. Figuring out a problem.

King Art's Kingdom. Castle celebrates...

"I've become king. With it, I've called a party to find my queen." King Art said.

"You've danced with all the girls. Only girl that's left is your cousin Caressa. Can't make her your wife?" Knight Verman said.

"Dance around from, and back to your partner." Knight Keen smiled in celebration.

"Love, that one?" Knight Verman didn't understand dance.

"Ha? Why you're not dancing." Knight Keen said.

"And, you." Knight Verman said.

"Haha?" Knight keen and Verman laughed. "Ha." They sighed.

"Will you dance with me, Caressa?" King Art joined the dance group again.

"You'll dance to Emma." Caressa put her hand out with laugh as she dances around from a guy to her cousin.

"That's my plan." King Art took her hand and danced with his cousin.

"Art, can't expect Emma who's investigating you, for that crown on your head, to marry you?" Caressa said.

"I was hoping Emma might not accept to become queen. Not while I'm under this crown." King Art said.

"Art, I don't understand?" Caressa asked. "You've worn the crown, they've accepted you, as their king?"

"Thanks for accepting to dance with a king, cousin." King Art let Caressa's hand go to another guy, taking Emma's hand, a next dance partner.

"Why have you circled around to me, skipping every other girl?" Emma asked. *"You knew, an investigation, doesn't have to get this close?"*

"Maybe, even a king has a right to party without being king for a night?" King Art asked.

"All right, we'll forget you've stolen a crown for tonight." Emma agreed. *"But, then how will you get your queen? Accept to become your queen, King Art?"*

"Ooh, that hurt, Emma. We were in that kitchen, longer than you'd like to admit, as friends?" King Art said.

"Then, you appeared to have a heart, of a knight." Emma said.

"But, what do you mean by it?" King Art asked.

"Maybe, that was the better man. Excuse me, I'm still on duty." Emma walked away.

"My king, make me your queen?" Maren danced around to King Art.

"Hm?" King Art saw Emma disappear in the crowd. *"I'm sorry, the song has ended."* King Art kissed Maren's hand and walked away.

"Has, he chosen you?" Friends ran to Maren.

"No, he hasn't chosen anyone." Maren looked toward the door where Emma had walked out a castle.

"I'm sorry." Caressa looked at her.

"It's, uhm, all right." Maren walked away.

"Haha." Maren's friends also walked away.

Knights Keen and Verman talk while having a drink...

"Might I join you, with a drink?" King Art asked himself front of the knights.

"Not, while looking for your queen, my king?" Knight Verman smiled.

"My king, has the girl you've chosen for queen, denied you?" Knight Keen asked. "Emma."

"It's all right, King Art, once you become king you've lost your chance with half the girls." Verman said.

"Why's that?" King Art asked.

"You've become king, of course." Knight Verman said.

"Don't worry, you still have half of them, to choose from." Knight Keen reminded.

"Maren. Would have liked to dance her around." Knight Verman said.

"But, we're not king." Knight Keen said.

"Ha, think she cares none." Knight Verman said.

"Ha?" Knight Keen and Verman laughed.

"Hm?" King Art watched Emma walk out a castle.

There are more celebrations. King Santino's castle. Days before in Queen Astrid's room...

"You've called, for a celebration of our love." Queen Astrid said. "But you will not allow they find out, the widow, has forgotten, you were her king's best friend?"

"We'll, not dance, together." King Santino said.

"But, my king?" Queen Astrid said. "They will find out anyway?" She turned away.

"You'll dance, with everyone." King Santino said. "I will, not ask you dance with me. They will believe, what they'd like. When they have, then we'll allow them find out, we have fallen in love?"

"You've forgotten war?" Queen Astrid asked.

"I've, uhm?" King Santino didn't answer. "For my queen, I did." King Santino kissed her.

"But, you haven't?" Queen Astrid turned away.

"I, uhm, ah?" King Santino sighed.

"I'll need you out my castle, my kingdom, my life?" Queen Astrid cried.

"But, my queen, it is you, who is in my—" King Santino said.

"Then, I'll take my things?" Queen Astrid cried.

"I did, go talk to King Randy, as we'd agreed. Only King Randy, has thought to take over the world?" King Santino said.

"The world? Has he any idea who exactly is, the world?" Queen Astrid nodded.

"But, our own?" King Santino shook his head.

"Ah?" They looked at each other.

"I like our world, lots better too." Knight Dario walked in the room. "I'm sorry, the door was open? The king has accepted to meet, meeting of kings. Only, if you attend?"

"But, King Randy has denied to have any peace talks, with King Santino?" Queen Astrid said.

"Looks like we better hurry a meeting?" Knight Dario said. "With, King Lance that is."

"Of course, we know, with what king?" Queen Astrid said.

"My Queen, I know you mourn, but you will attend, a meeting?" Knight Dario asked.

"I, uhm, had King Reymundo attend them, when well, he hadn't started war." Queen Astrid said. "I suppose, you will allow my word be heard, King Santino?"

"But, my queen?" King Santino said. "I'm not one to speak for you?"

"Hm?" Knight Dario turning away without looking away watched them talk, waiting for answer.

"I, suppose, I must, attend?" Queen Astrid said.

"Thank you, Queen Astrid, my King Lance appreciates, a queen of your kind." Knight Dario said and walked away. "Peaceful."

"You'll see, how these talks are, my queen." King Santino said.

"My Santino, you have tried?" Queen Astrid held his hand.

"Ah?" They looked around the castle made sure no one was around.

"Is it we've fallen in love?" Queen Astrid asked.

"Is it?" King Santino kissed her.

At the party...

"They can't deny something is going on between them?" Summer an invite said.

"That'll probably be true, couple more days spent in this castle together. But, Reymundo did know to trust his best friend King Santino." Sam another of the ladies said.

"Will you dance, with me?" King Randy put his hand out to Queen Astrid.

"Hm?" King Santino steps away watching them got a wine glass from a tray someone carried.

"Ah?" Queen Astrid looked at King Santino too.

"Ah?" King Santino put his drink up to Queen Astrid.

"Hm." Queen Astrid smiled accepting to dance with King Randy.

"You, and the king, is it, you have started something more than friendship?" King Randy danced with Queen Astrid. "Allow they skip us, when they come around to take you from me?"

"Is it they will come looking for you?" Queen Astrid asked King Randy dancing to center creating a couples' dance floor.

"Hm, a royals' dance." King Randy smiled. "If King Santino hasn't proposed anything, may I?"

"May I?" King Santino was side of them.

"You, may?" King Randy asked for Queen Astrid's approval.

"Ah?" Queen Astrid nodded.

"Thank you, my queen?" King Randy took a stepped back.

"You said, we wouldn't dance—" Queen Astrid danced with King Santino.

"I think it's enough time?" King Randy said. "You've figured yourself out dance with others?"

"It was his idea?" Queen Astrid said. "Maybe, he knows something. He's trying, I don't know, make you understand—"

"Not to start a war?" King Santino asked. "I've understood that. But I will start a war, if anyone gets anywhere, near you. For any other reason than, dance?"

"I, will decide on that." Queen Astrid walked away.

"My queen?" King Santino followed her pulling her arm toward him.

"You're hurting me?" Queen Astrid looked at his hand holding her arm.

"You've hurt me, leaving me on the dance floor?" King Santino looked around at everyone watching them with smile. "Let's not make a scene, it's one already? We've danced." He smiled at everyone.

"Hm?" Queen Astrid looked around. "Very well, we'll have peace talks, again?" She said as people passed by chatting.

"Yes, peace talks?" King Santino said. "Think, they'll believe, it's what we talk about?"

"Haha?" Queen Astrid giggled.

"Ha?" They all whispered around them.

"Hm?" Both King and Queen smiled.

"I told you, they have one thing in mind. That's, rule the world." Sam told her friend as they passed Queen and King.

"Peace, is it they talk?" Summer asked. "Do, remember a widow of war."

"Ah?" Sam and Summer looked at each other. "Haha?"

"I'll, uhm, move from your castle, as soon as—" Queen Astrid said.

"I've only invited them to a celebration, but it's been marriage. My surprise?" King Santino asked still holding her hand.

"Oh?" Queen Astrid nodded in cry. "Aha."

"I'll give you the ring, when everyone's left." King Santino kissed Astrid's hand and let it go.

"What do you suppose they are whispering to each other's ear now?" Sam asked.

"Haven't an idea?" Sam said.

"Haha." Friends enjoyed celebration.

"Girls, enjoying the party?" King Randy asked.

"Have you chosen a wife?" Summer asked loudly.

"Think, the whole world of kings has, found them out." King Randy smiled with whisper.

"You will, agree to peace talks, why you're here?" Summer asked.

"Ah?" King Randy smiled.

"Tell me, King Randy, is there any honor code between those three crowns?" Summer asked.

"Oh, you leave the king alone, he might begin talking peace, now?" Sam smiled at Summer.

"I like you, Sam." King Randy held her hand and kissed it.

"Hm, ah?" Sam ran her finger down his hand as he continued to hold her hand front of him.

"Ah, Sam?" Summer elbowed her. "Do remember he's, uhm, King Randy?"

"Hm?" King Randy looked at Summer.

"Hm?" Summer smiled at him then looked at Sam.

"My lady, I will leave you to your friend. Perhaps, I'll call you sometime?"

"Ah?" Sam put her hand out to him. "Do?" She pulled her hand near to her face.

"Sam?" Summer asked pulling her hand down to her side. "You can't possibly be serious? Now what would you want with a man, like that?"

"Ah?" Sam did keep secret with smile.

"Think, he will?" Summer scold with a wine glass in her hands. "Have nothing more than—

"Peace talks." Sam did smile.

After a celebration...

"We are still in time to be together, before a war?" King Santino knelt, held an open box with a ring front of Queen Astrid in her room.

"Yes." Queen Astrid nodded taking the ring. "I'll be your queen." She put the ring on.

"Let's just hope, King Lance, will figure out enough time for our wedding?" King Santino held her hands front of them.

"Oh, Santino?" Queen Astrid cried kissing him.

"We're on borrowed time." King Santino kissed her.

King Santino is in trouble?

"Queen Astrid has asked she be excused for obvious reasons?" King Santino was in a meeting room.

"A queen might shine, with her absence." King Lance said.

"Without a queen's word, might it be, something's not been said?" King Randy asked. "Keep us wondering, is what a queen does?"

"Ah?" King Santino looked at him.

"Let us begin a meeting. Why is it you war, King Santino?" King Lance must ask, King Santino.

"You mean initially? Said peace talks? My kingdom, is now two crowns. My wife and mine. And, we'll need a bigger kingdom." King Santino explained.

"Ha, you'd think a king's crown, would afford, a queen's treasure." King Randy looked at the kings then at King Santino. "Make even more, on its own?" He questioned. "Is it she, affords you?"

"King Randy, let us not be enemies?" King Santino asked. "But would it been with your, crown?"

"Hm?" Randy didn't answer.

...

"Oh, but once you're done trying to end my kingdom, you will see what a real war, is." King Randy smiled with a wine glass in his hand.

"You're not threatening, my King Randy?" King Santino asked.

"In love, in war?" King Randy did answer. "Anything goes?"

"Now what will your purpose, with that be?" King Santino asked. "When I've understood, I've lost kings', uhm, friendship starting war."

"That, I might end with a won crown, unlike your best friend, King Reymundo." King Randy said. "And, your unfinished war."

"What makes you so sure, I won't finish this war?" King Santino asked. "If, you continue fight with me?"

"Oh, but you forget, my kings?" King Lance in a meeting of kings in his castle asked. "Too be in war with one crown, is to ask war from all crowns?"

"Hm?" Both king Santino and king Randy turned to look at him.

"To be in war with me, is to ask war with me." King Randy reminded. "You, all?"

"Allow me, rephrase that?" King Lance apologized. "To begin a war, with anyone, for no reason at all, but fortune? Is to lose our alliance, to you."

"Hm?" King Santino looked at King Lance. "Ha?" He questioned King Randy. "Well. I've called it unfinished business."

"Thank you." King Lance said. "Two crowns in war brought together in my kingdom, for the sole purpose, of peace." He smiled.

"Oh, but we've not talked, a second part of a plan?" King Art must tell.

"Ah?" King Lance must hear it.

"Think our king, King Lance has had enough for today?" King Randy looked at King Lance. "Allow, he continue a meeting, next time?" He asked King Art.

"But this is important?" King Art said.

"Everything, is important when a meeting of kings, King Art. Only, King Randy is right, might we leave this for another meeting?" King Lance said.

"King Randy, do you continue to be part of, A World Ruled By Kings?" King Santino asked.

"Ah?" King Randy, might he answer?

"My King Lance, I wouldn't bother you the same. King Randy, might you allow you tell in which way you're a loyal crown, to World Ruled By Kings?" King Art must speak.

"Might I begin, with reminder of how we aren't all loyal friends here?" King Randy asked. "From one king wanting to be big brother, to a king that's stolen his own best friend's widow, before he died?"

"Ah?" They all looked at each other.

"Might it be, King Warren has taken other secrets to his grave, must it be, I chose to quiet about them?" King Randy

asked. "With this, I'll explain how you've done nothing but broken yourselves; A World Ruled By Kings. My only intention is to bring it back together."

"How, King Randy, is it you intend to do, this?" King Lance asked.

"By making it one crown." King Randy said.

"But, you can't be serious?" King Lance said. "You know, despite all that's happened, we won't allow any other crown fall?" He looked at all the kings.

"Hm, ah?" They argued.

"Won't, you?" King Randy watched them argue too.

"Remind ourselves, you are," King Lance asked. "kings."

"Hm. Ah?" They mumbled.

"We, my King Lance," King Randy reminded with interruption. "are, kings. King can't rule without having blood on his hands."

"I'd say, what we don't know about you, King Lance, but you've more than showed us your true character." King Santino stood front of him looking down at his shoes. "Hm." He looked up at him.

And sometime later...

"My king, I must tell you," King Santino walked in King Lance's office. "King Randy has begun war against me?"

"What purpose?" King Lance asked.

"I'd like to finish what, neither king Reymundo, nor King Santino did." King Randy said.

"Hm?" King Santino looked at him. "But, you've won a war, without starting it. There's nothing to prove."

"I'd still would like to rule the world?" King Randy said.

"We live in a place, called A World Ruled By Kings. Ruled by peace. Surely, you know, there's a world out there, that will come assist us, if we call?" King Lance reminded.

"They will save their war, for a real war." King Randy knew.

"You can't be serious? You can't war against us? You'll bring your old enemy, King Santino against you, he's called this meeting, to let us all know?" King Lance is in a meeting.

"Very, well. We're in war. I'll tell you how this will go down." King Randy said. "I'll bring down, one crown at a time, until all your crowns are mine, I'll have one kingdom. Sure, it's been tried before? But this time, I assure you, will work. Being that you all are against me, because I'm coming after each won kingdom. After yours King Lance, there is still one kingdom that has nor crown, but loyal? Gypsies, will be allowed, to bring up their cloak from their face."

"But King Randy, you do remember? It was I, who asked, they cover their face with their cloak. Understanding, they have a king? Then, it won't be you, but I, who has asked they bring down their cloak off their face." King Lance made a command to one of his knights. "A king, they've had."

"Right away." A knight had received a message and walked out the office.

"You, dare, call yourself their, king?" King Randy asked. "You, my king, must understand this is a real war. And, one day, you too will turn in your crown, with your people. See, we both *know, when a war, we lose, our knights. I'm sure, nor your kings, nor you, would like to lose, any more, to me?"*

"Hm?" They all looked at each other and at him.

"Whichever kingdom agrees to turn in your crown, will be under my cover, from war. But, will have accepted to be, the knight to war, for me against those who have rebelled with disobedience accepting new king?" King Randy advised.

"Ah?" Kings looked at each other.

"Don't forget I only look to unite every crown, that has found reason for quarrel against each other, with my own." King Randy said. "It's a fight, to regain peace."

"If you ever had secret code? Against, Randy?" King Art did ask with whisper next to King Lance in a castle's meeting room.

"Unity, has never been secrecy. War must never be, game of chess." King Lance spoke front of kings.

"Ah?" Kings looked at each other.

"Hm." Kings Lance and Randy looked at each other.

The war began. One crown was lost, then another. The kings lost men. Losing their crown. King Randy won war and another...

"I don't understand, we've lost a crown. I thought we had a queen, who looked up, more than to a crown? If, King Randy continues on with triumph, we'll have lost A World Ruled By Kings, forever. A world ruled by, an iron hand?" Santino is in his home. He's lost a castle.

"I'm sure the queen, hasn't shown to meetings, because she's become busy, trying to stop war." Knight Dario said.

"Knight Dario, what is it you do here?" Santino asked.

"King Lance, would like you to know he's sorry he's failed his attempt to help you out a war." Knight Dario said. "He'd also like you to know, he won't stop, until King Randy realizes, unity may only be brought by peace not war."

"Knight Dario, remind King Lance, King Randy is unlike no other." Santino put his hand on Knight Dario's shoulder.

"We've found out." Knight Dario walked out his house.

King Randy brought down many men, and more men until everyone gave in their crown. He had one last crown to get and he'd turn A World Ruled By Kings, into, King of Worlds...

"I've not tire to war." King Lance a last king to defeat said. "You all know how it feels to lose a horse in the game of chess."

"Hm?" They all looked at each other.

"Not willing to lose one more of my men, if I may avoid it?" King Lance said. "You will kneel loyal to a crown, under a sword. Knowing you only serve, but one king."

"Hm?" They all looked at each other.

"My last attempt to save you." King Lance took of his crown and put it in a crystal box in his meeting room.

"Ah?" They mumbled a final lost crown.

At King Randy's castle. In a king's office...

"My king, we have a special gift for you?" Knight Dario walked in the castle with a crystal boxed gift.

"My king, this was too easy, do think accepting it?" One of King Randy's knights asked.

"I assure you, the king's intention is only to save his horse, from a game of chess?" Knight Dario explained still holding a crown to the king.

"King Lance has turned in his kingdom." King Randy did accept with a smile.

"My, king." Knight Dario was front of him.

"Knight." King Lance turned around and put a crown next to others. "I want a new crown, made from each of these crowns."

"My king." One of his men said looking at other knights.

"Now." King Randy asked.

"The strength of a king, are six crowns." Knight Dario said.

"Ah?" King Randy looked at him. Might he trust, knight Dario?

Santino has found out the news. He is in Lance's home…

"King Randy has won the war, King Lance." Santino walked in Lance's now home. "I can't say, I don't understand a game of chess."

"The queen has been missed." Lance said.

"Forgiven? Perhaps King Randy thinks, a queen may be romanced out crown." Santino looked at a fireplace.

"Ah?" Lance looked at Santino.

"I know. I'm out on the street, without a crown. Might I still give, command?" Lance once a king said.

"There might be a way to get our crowns back?" Santino wasn't giving up.

"We want to hear it?" The others who'd lost a crown were also In Lance's home.

"Sorry, I didn't notice you there." Santino turned back to look at them.

"We're still having meetings?" King Lance said. "Over how, we're a lost crown."

"Ha?" They laughed.

"We are?" Art, Jakens, and Zodek who was crowned king of King Warren's kingdom said.

"One day, we were all kings. Our knights, knew when we talk to them, what we meant. If we all talk to our own knights, they will instead fight a real war." King Lance said.

"Turning against each other?" Knight Art reminded loyalty to one's king.

"Fighting one war, one enemy, a real war?" Santino said. "That will be the message?"

"But, being that they were our men, with a new king now? Even if they recognize, each other as whose men they once were? How will they know whose sword each other, serve?" King Art asked. "An old sword, a new?"

"Ah?" They all mumbled.

"We must have faithful men, between a war, that's been won." Santino said. *"They will, war against a real enemy. King Randy will have no choice, but to return our kingdoms. He'll lose, his own men. Faithful. Surely, a king may have men, but not all faithful?"*

"Because they still serve a loyal crown." Lance said.

"This makes no sense." Zodek said.

"Ah?" Everyone turned to look a Zodek.

"Whose side are you on?" King Santino asked.

"This will not be easy. Remember, we've given up crown, to save knight." Zodek reminded. *"Maybe, good king win?"*

King Randy's Kingdom. And so, knights talk...

"New crowns, to my crown. I have many who rebel. Get rid of the rebels, unwilling to serve every command the king might have." King Randy asked.

"We too, are unwilling to serve your every command. Might want to send us to the kitchen?" Knight Keen said.

"Dario, you know what to do, with rebels?" King Randy didn't look at Knight Keen.

"Knight Keen, the dungeon is a castle favorite. If you don't want to serve, a king?" Knight Dario was front of Knight Keen with command.

"Knight Keen, will you do as I ask. Make sure a king keeps his all-in-one crown?" King Randy insisted about command.

"Hm!" Knight Keen looked at Knight Dario.

"Hm?" Knight Dario looked at Knight Keen with plead.

Outside a castle...

"Guys, have a knew king now." Knight Dario walked to some knights front of a castle.

"You're loyal as can be, to your King Randy. You've become traitor!" Knight Keen yelled.

"There's a reason for my betrayal?" Knight Dario had joined a kingdom.

"Couldn't escape it. We've both become traitors." Knight Verman reminded knight keen.

"Hm?" Knight Keen knew.

"We recognize each as another's king's men. Can't allow us be divided, by one king?" Knight Verman asked.

"Right, we should recognize one crown, the right one." Knight Dario said. "That's the only way we'll get that crown right."

"Whose king?" Knight keen asked.

"Knight Lance." Knight Dario said. "They said, each of you would recognize the words, and obey. Tell each of your men, it's become time."

"Serve, one crown, one command." Knights understood the command.

"But they say, the queen, has overruled any command, will save us?" Knight Verman said to the knights circled around.

"What, queen?" They all asked.

"What's going on here?" King's knight walked over to the knights.

"Nothing." They all got in posture.

"What is it, you boys gather to talk about?" Knight Rhett one of king Randy's men asked. "Thought we were, one crown?"

"We, are." Knight Dario assured. "Just talking. How we should make sure, we're all good." He looked with command at Knight Keen.

"King's order." Knight Keen said.

"Get to doing something?" Knight Rhett asked.

"What else is there to do? We've won, the war. No other kingdoms ruled by any other kings, anymore. One king, now." Knight Keen said. "King of Worlds."

"You better not be planning anything." Knight Rhett said. "Not when through war, we've found peace?"

"It's all we wanted. Why we knelt to that sword." Knight Keen said.

"You're not being a smart guy, Keen? Know you smarter than that." Knight Rhett said.

"He's not." Knight Guy said. "You see us a contrary knight, with the queen marrying, a best friend's, wife? After his death?"

"Hm? Ah." Randy's knight Rhett walked away.

"Thanks, Guy." Knight Keen thanked.

"You'll find a way to thank me, later." Knight Guy walked away.

"I don't want to join your party." Knight Mitch another of King Randy's loyal men said. "This has been my kingdom, since King Reymundo. Get it, why you're unwilling to forgive. But, we're all in this? If we can forget war, and have peace. Why not have it?" He held his sword in place. "Aren't, we really all, one? Because we want, peace?"

"Hm?" They all looked at each other. "Ah?" They were all in disagreement.

"We, all must be divided, for our own king's sake." Knight Keen said.

"Yeah." Knight Verman agreed. "We'll end up serving, King Randy forever? Not sure, he won't do this again? Another, World Ruled By Kings?"

"Those worlds, are ruled by giants." Knight Guy walked over to them again. "Think, King Randy knows that."

"King Randy he's become one himself." Knight Keen said.

"How will we do this?" Knight Verman asked. "I much rather, think Art is our king, than serve King Randy one more day? Maybe, fighting each other as though two opposing crowns, so we can have our own king back, isn't the plan? But, planning, this escape, like we never were enemies?"

"Remember, instead, how once, we were friends?" Knight Keen also spoke. "But one enemy, and enemy is within us, we within them?"

"Ha?" Everyone began arguing.

"Hm!" Knight Mitch looked at them. "Hate to think the rest of my men dead?" He was leader of knights. "Why, you'll come after us? You know, we'll lose a war like that?

Outnumbered. You're all made up of, how many kingdoms? Supposed to be one, but looks like the king didn't think it through, and instead has made himself, same enemies? No matter what it looks like?" He saw betrayal.

"Hm?" They all looked at him.

"Be careful, with me?" Knight Mitch asked. "When, you all wonder about whose knight each other is to what king? My king has an exact idea, of who you knelt to once? Too, I recognize the men, who served here, before all you traitors, knelt fake alliance?"

"Ah?" They all looked at each other.

"I'm not going to stop you." Knight Mitch said. "But, I do remind you, it's not war, you're looking for. So, if you want to escape, a king? Don't come after his knights. A war, has ended. Least, King Randy's real knights, understood, just that." He walked away.

"Might want to exclude him from, our next meeting?" Knight Keen looked at a group of knights still mumbling.

"Ha?" Some knights laughed.

"Excluding us, would only give King Randy reason to fear, betrayal." One of King Randy's knights, knight Azuer reminded. "You've only rumored, war threat. Without secrecy."

"But, you all do know, who the rebels, of such war, are?" Knight Dario did speak. "In which case, King Randy knows, knights who betray."

"Right, knight Dario, King Randy would only suspect us, before his knew loyal knight." Knight Azuer understood. "Might King Randy find betrayal, on time?"

"Oh, but whose knight am I," Knight Dario stood front of knight Azuer. "really?" He smiled.

"Ah?" Knight Azuer said nothing.

"Am I just finding out, about betrayal, from all kings and kings' men?" Knight Dario looked at everyone.

"Hm, ah?" Everyone looking at knight Dario mumbled within them.

"Hm?" Knight Azuer looked at knight Dario as if studying him.

"Ah?" Knight Dario was front of everyone who continued with mumble.

A book, but life must continue...

"Mona?" Art is in her office.

"Yes?" Mona turned her attention from a computer to Art at her desk.

"I'd like to know how my war ends?" Art asked.

"Astrid, responsible queen about her own fortune..." Mona smiled. "Meets Randy in one of those king parties. Since, the world, really is a world ruled by kings, Randy's heart melts for Queen Astrid. His heart is changed."

"But the kings," Art asked. "such, as myself, we've lost a crown?"

"Great all you are, move out that, King of Worlds, make of a new kingdom out in this world." Mona smiled.

"Now, why is it called, Precious Gems again?" Art asked.

"Takes precious gems to stop a war from happening." Mona said. "Gypsy did unite at one point, and with the most high king. Let's call him Mr. McDudley. Somethings like peace, doesn't have price, Art."

"Now, for a last question. Will we be turning in our own crown?" Art asked front of her middle of an office.

"Is it, for family?" Mona asked. "Yes, I believe we've been overruled."

"I was afraid to ask?" Art said.

"Haha. Get started on that next story." Mona said.

"Mona, why is it you didn't care to turn in that story, Precious Gems?" Art asked. "Is it, love?"

"Guy has ruled our world. Art, you forget, I have my own contracts." Mona was at her desk.

"Hm. Got it." Art walked out the office.

"How's that haunt?" Mona saw Somra walk in the door.

"It's, uhm, unfinished business." Somra said.

"Somra, is all unfinished business, meant to be finished?" Mona asked.

"Ah, I might want to ask for time, to answer that one?" Somra said.

"Take all the time you need." Mona said.

An end of a book...

"Queen Astrid." King Randy welcomed in his office. "I've asked my men, to recognize a queen, when front of them."

"Thank you, King Randy." Queen Astrid smiled. "King Randy, why have you allowed my crown escape? Is it, I'm a queen not a king?"

"Your crown, will serve along with mine." King Randy walked to her. "And your crown has not resisted to any of my orders?"

"Even a king wouldn't have resisted." Queen Astrid said. "We'll get around to talking unfair?"

"Have you noticed, your men, along with others, they continue to respect your crown?" King Randy said.

"Is it, respect, not fear, I've conquered?" Queen Astrid asked.

"Will you, now that you've lost your king, marry me? Least, won't call this, betrayal to a, friend?" King Randy kissed her hand.

"Hm?" Queen Astrid watched him. She didn't answer.

"Sometimes, when a crown weighs, one must put their head down," Queen Astrid walked to a balcony but didn't go outside. "for the sake not only of one's self, but for family." She turned around and looked at King Randy.

"For, one's family." King Randy said.

"King Randy, is it peace talks, with the queen?" Giana walked in the office.

"As women, we will talk peace?" Queen Astrid asked Giana.

"But, you are queen. A girl like me, could never war against you." Giana said.

"Thank you for understanding that, Giana." Queen Astrid smiled.

"Giana, meet your knew queen. Queen Astrid will have a crown over hers to rule with." King Randy said.

"Ah?" Giana watched their stares. "I, uhm, will get dinner ready?"

"Thank you." King Randy smiled.

"Excuse, me." Giana walked out the door.

"Would you like to walk a garden, meanwhile dinner is ready?" King Randy asked.

"I'd love to." Queen Astrid put her hand up to a side of her.

"Hm." King Randy held it and walked with her out the door.

"I believe, King Randy's plan has worked." King Mitch in the hallway watched a couple go downstairs.

"Plan to, what?" Knight Keen was in the hallway.

"You take a crown from a king, a queen will agree to date, a king." Knight Mitch said.

"All this time I thought, was Dario's plan." Knight Keen smiled.

"What for?" Knight Mitch asked.

"King Santino mustn't marry the wrong girl." Knight Keen said.

"Ah?" Knight Mitch asked. "Wrong girl?"

"Queen Astrid, will marry and again." Knight Verman said.

"When one's found the right king?" Knight Mitch went downstairs.

"You don't really think Queen Astrid's heart, neither a crown is owned by a man?" Knight Keen asked.

"Ah, no." Knight Verman assured. "Some queens, but owe themselves, to their kingdom."

"Hm?" Knight Guy is in the hallway.

In the Garden...

"Queen Astrid?" Knight Guy is in the garden.

"Knight Guy?" Queen Astrid asked. "Your king has sent you look for me?"

"No, I've come to look for you myself." Knight Guy assured.

"What is the reason for it?" Queen Astrid had a garden's rose in her hand.

"I may ask you to join me for dinner tonight?" Knight Guy asked.

"You are Santino's brother, I know now?" Queen Astrid said.

"That would have been all wrong of me, to ask you, before you knew that about me?" Knight Guy said.

"That I've found out, doesn't deny the fact, you're his brother?" Queen Astrid said.

"You will, have dinner with me?" Knight Guy asked.

"My queen, forgive me for my affairs?" King Randy walked to join Queen Astrid again in the Garden.

"I've found knight Guy in my walk." Queen Astrid apologized.

"Knight Guy, I don't consider you enemy, when you serve the king." King Randy acknowledged Knight Guy. "But, I must warn, a queen must be taken care of, like queen."

"Hm?" Knight Guy looked at her.

"And, I remind you, as though you'd forgotten, one mustn't disrespect a woman, by dating her, after his own brother?" King Randy said.

"Oh, but the world in disagreement, of conquered love?" Knight Guy said. "Astrid, forgive me, if my courtship has disrespected, you."

"Ah?" Queen Astrid looked at him.

"Dinner, is ready, as you like it." King Randy took her arm.

"Thank you, my king." Queen Astrid walked away with the king.

"Hm, ah?" Knight Guy looked around in the garden. "My queen?" He sighed.

"Oh, but will she be." Knight Mitch was in the garden.

"Ah?" Knight Guy looked at him.

"A knight, Guy, but are you willing to die, for the queen?" Knight Mitch asked.

"Oh, but, when a queen asks for peace." Knight Guy walked away.

"Hm. Ah?" Knight Mitch's mouth dropped.

Time before. Some people share a room...

"Tell me, Sumae, why does it feel like I wake up to a war every day?" Emma woke up sitting up in her bed.

"Because, we do wake up to war every day." Sumae Emma's roommate also woke up sitting up in her bed.

"Don't we look lovely this morning?" Mona turned to look at Sumae in her bed next to hers.

"Ha? Don't we?" Sumae dragged her feet to the restroom. *"Will, in a bit."* She looked in the mirror brushing her teeth.

"Haha." Emma braided her hair at a mirror in the bedroom.

Emma and Sumae are called to Queen Mona's office. In Mona's Castle, in the office...

"One last sentence, girls?" Mona wrote at her desk.

"Mona busy at her office." Emma and Sumae waited for Mona in the office.

"Haha. Thank you, girls, for joining a meeting." Mona laughed in her office. *"Bring Art to me, ladies. You've completed an investigation."*

At what used to be King Art's castle...

"Queen has asked I bring you back to her kingdom, to pay for your fault. Stealing a crown." Emma said. *"You've taken

a crown that doesn't belong to you. And, with it, to rule a kingdom, that was never to be. That is, ruled by very little law."

"Emma, might you want to listen, before you bring me to your Queen, Mona?" King Art took his crown off. "With Queen Astrid's plead for some kind of peace, King Randy has allowed I keep, but ruins and its crown. Must we continue to wait on your Queens, rule?"

"I'll listen, but my partner, Sumae, is very impatient." Emma looked to the door.

"Hm." Sumae put her hand to her forehead and down side of her.

"I've only taken a crown, to return it." Art said.

"May, I ask to who?" Emma asked.

"You." Art gave Emma the crown.

"What?" Verman and Keen yelled.

"Crown. Would be beginning of something?" Keen cried.

"Well, King Randy has denied any more kingdoms?" Verman sighed.

"Maybe we should fall in love, you know, not with each other, but in love?" Keen said.

"Ooh, I better watch it with you?" Verman said.

"Wide awake. You watch it, now." Keen said.

"Hey!" Verman yelled offended.

"Hey!" Keen yelled offended.

"Haha." Emma and Art laughed.

"We'll forget a kingdom, with love?" Keen looked to Art and Emma.

"You'll forgive me now?" Art asked Emma.

"Ah?" Emma held the crown in her hand.

Back at Queen Mona's Castle...

"Emma, holding evidence of a stolen crown." Queen Mona walked to Emma. *"Sumae, what have you got to say about this one?"*

"I, ah?" Sumae tried to say.

"My queen, may I explain?" Emma asked.

"I doubt, you will have any valid explanation?" Queen Mona asked.

"I've only stolen a crown, but to return it?" Emma said.

"True, story?" Sumae said.

"Haha." Queen Mona laughed. *"Thank you, girls. Mission complete. The crown has been returned to its rightful, owner."* She studied the crown in her hands.

"Hm?" Emma and Sumae looked at each other. *"Ha?"* They smiled.

"Haha. Think you girls, deserve your own room now." Mona laughed with the crown in her hands.

Back at what used to be Art's castle...

"Time before all this is taken away, you had a party in this castle." Verman said.

"Yes, and you asked every girl to dance, so you would find your queen." Keen said. "What was the whole point of that one. You even danced with, your cousin Caressa?"

"None, of the girls, were the chosen to be your queen. No, now you don't even have a crown. Tell me, what the whole point of giving it away, was?" Keen asked.

"If, all goes well, you'll see, why?" Art said.

"Art?" Emma walked in the castle.

"Emma, you've returned?" Art stood up from castle stairs.

"What is this? I thought you were in love with Queen Mona?" Keen asked.

"You don't know a whole story." Verman said.

"I, thought you a thief?" Emma apologized. "Why, I didn't want to dance with you, that night. Though, that crown almost felt like we could be royals together, forever?"

"Haha?" Art laughed. "Now, will you dance with me, Emma?"

"There's no music?" Emma said.

"Haha." Art and Emma laughed.

"Hm, well hurry! We don't have much time in this castle, before its rightful owner, comes ask for it?" Verman asked Keen.

"I got music?" Keen played music.

"Will you, be my queen, Emma?" Art asked her to dance.

"I waited all my life for my, king." Emma took Art's hand.

"Now, that's a reason for a lost crown." Keen said.

"Well, it's, uhm, real love, Keen. Nothing you'd understand?" Verman said.

"I understand real love. It's got nothing to do with money." Keen said. "Oh, but of course you tricked me into saying that.

"Was, no trick?" Verman said. "Looks like we've found our king and queen."

"Not the kind we want." Keen said.

"All right, party over. Haha. Says here, I own it all." Queen Mona walked in the castle with documents.

Moments from the past...

"Mona, I'd like you and Art to live your life, happy. I've told Art, he may enjoy that phone call, his life with you now." Desmon said.

"I don't see why you'd do that, Desmon." Mona smiled. "Last time, matches to time now. Haha. Art, will never call again. If he only knew, I'd say yes."

"Hm?" Desmon watched her as he reached into his pocket.

"To that, ring." Mona said.

"Haha." They laughed.

"Allow, I tell Loretta my best friend, I'm on a date?" Desmon answered a phone call.

"You may?" Mona looked at him. "Forgot you had a girlfriend Mona, danced with Loretta? Went to that party without me?" She dare ask over Desmon's conversation.

"Hm?" Desmon looked at her hanging up a phone. "Mona, this isn't any date."

"No, it's not." Mona put her napkin on her plate. "You've just answered another girl's phone call."

"I assure, unlike Art, that's just a friend." Desmon smiled. "We're here together, it's a special date."

At another table...

"Mona, don't forget, I've allowed Desmon get back to you." Loretta said to herself. She drank from her glass. She watched the couple talk and laugh. "You owe me more than you'd like."

"Loretta, thanks for meeting with me." Mr. Scavo sat at the table. "Now, about that fighting?"

"Fighting, there's no one fighting." Loretta assured Mr. Scavo.

"Loretta, I've heard...?" Mr. Scavo watched another table.

"Something wrong, Mr. Scavo?" Loretta asked. "Is it, Mona having dinner with Desmon? Ooh, I've ended a war. But you'll help me win it back?"

"Ah?" Mr. Scavo turned his attention to Loretta again. "I don't know what you're talking about?"

"Don't you, Mr. Scavo?" Loretta smiled.

"Mona and I, no matter what you've heard, it's all business." Mr. Scavo said.

"You'll say that about every girl, that's been close to you in your office." Loretta said.

"Wrong, Loretta, you'd like to forget, my wife Vienna." Mr. Scavo said.

"Ah?" Loretta said nothing.

Desmon and Mona enjoy dinner in a restaurant. Another date?

"Mona, we've had many dates. I enjoy every one of them. Never a dull moment with you." Desmon smiled.

"Haha." Mona laughed. *"It's what everyone says?"*

"But, this date isn't like any other. Not for me, nor for you." Desmon smiled reaching into his pocket at a dinner table. *"Sweating it."* He wiped his face with a napkin from his pocket.

"Dessert?" A waiter walked to their table.

"I shouldn't." Mona said with a shook of her head.

"Oh, but this one isn't just dessert?" The waiter put his hand down to her.

"Ah?" Mona saw a cheesecake with a ringed cherry was front of her.

"In case you're wondering, Mona--" Desmon smiled.

"Apart from conversations, we've had in a past? Not an... Desmon?" Mona shook her head with surprise still looking at the ring on the dessert.

"Thought, I'd get to that ring, before Art?" Desmon smiled.

"Oh, oh?" Mona was surprised. *"Ooh? Yes, yes, Desmon, yes!"*

"She's said, yes." Desmon saw everyone turned to look at their table.

"Aah?" Everyone cheered an engagement.

Present time at Seagull's ship...

"Mona, are you single?" A man asked front of a boat on boat rails.

"Yes, I am. I mean, now I am?" Mona said.

"You were, up on that third cloud for a moment?" The man asked. *"Is it scenery?"*

"Hm, ah?" Mona looked at him. *"I'm just not used to meeting complete strangers?"* Mona smiled.

"When a person falls in love, with another, it's usually because they're complete strangers?" The man said.

"Haha?" Mona and he laughed.

"Mona?" Guy walked to her. *"What part of, I'll be back, don't you understand?"*

"Haha." Mona laughed.

"Forgive a private conversation?" Guy asked. *"Hi, my name, is Guy?"*

"Guy?" The man looked at him. *"Mona?"*

"Private is what this should be?" Mona tried apologizing.

"Guy, you've forgotten Darla?" Sage walked to him.

"Dad." Guy son walked to them.

"Son?" Guy saw they weren't alone.

"Private conversation?" The man asked.

"Haha?" They laughed.

"Not as funny as I am, Guy?" Lance walked front of his ship. "I've found Darla somewhere in the ship. She was looking for her date?"

"Guy?" Darla walked to him. "I thought it was you and I?"

"And, I have no idea what I've just walked into?" The man said.

"Haha?" Everyone laughed.

At a bar knights Verman and Keen drink...

"One question remains?" Keen asked Verman in a bar.

"What's that?" Verman asked.

"Who's poisoned the king's food?" Knight Rhett sat at the bar with them.

"Rhett, weren't you cook, for King Jakens?" Keen pointed at him.

"Yes," Knight Rhett held the drink in his hand. "I was." He drank from his drink. But I must say, hate cooking. All that heat, just coming at you?"

"Ah?" Keen and Verman looked at each other.

"Know what that means, right?" Verman asked Keen.

"Have you caught on?" Knight Rhett asked guilty?

Katie edits…

"King Randy, under my direction you've agreed to return every crown to its rightful owner. Therefor bringing business back to, World Ruled By Kings. Is it, King Randy, the world might need to be ruled by, a queen?" Queen Mona asked. "You're much to good for this, King."

"I, uh, hm?" King Randy looked at Mona without an answer. "If a king might not do what he must for a world, might another king step in?"

"What is it, a king might do for its world?" Queen Mona asked. "I thought it, our job done?"

"Keep the world going round. God already does that, my King Randy." Queen Astrid walked in the office.

"Queen Astrid, thought you'd for sure gone back to your crowned King Santino?" Queen Mona asked.

"As you can see, Queen Mona, I have been under the command, of but one queen, Queen Astrid's." King Randy said. "I will marry her." King Randy said.

"Yes, of course, King Randy. An investigation has but ended? I will leave you alone to your life." Queen Mona walked out an office.

"I love you, Queen Astrid." King Randy was alone with Queen Astrid. "Might the question be, do you love me? Are you sure, it's me you'll marry?"

"My king? Why doubt me?" Queen Astrid asked.

The End